College House, 45, East Street, Faversham, Kent. Faversham 2302. March 10th 1979

BAKER'S DOZEN

BAKER'S DOZEN

A Collection of Stories

Edited by

LEON GARFIELD

Ward Lock Limited · London

ISBN 0 7063 1408 5

First published in Great Britain in 1973
by Ward Lock Limited, 116 Baker Street,
London, W1M 2BB

Reprinted 1976

Text set in 12 on 14 point Baskerville

Printed in Great Britain by
Willmer Brothers Limited, Birkenhead

CONTENTS

INTRODUCTION

Long ago, there were no books especially for the young except those from which they learned to read. Otherwise there were just books, written for whoever was interested in them. There was never any doubt as to who the books were for. There were learned books for those who wished to learn; there were political satires written by angry men; there were Utopias written by hopeful men; there were poems written by poets to minister to the dreams of all who bought them, and there were novels, or stories, written for the family. These novels were reckoned suitable for anyone who was able to read them. There was no question of an author sitting down to write books especially for the young reader. Nowadays, however, it's different, and a whole new industry has grown up of books for the young. Some of them are very good, but most of them have the stringency and bite of a wet nappy. This is because so many authors imagine that the young reader is not only simple in his tastes, but also simple in his mind. They write as though for three year olds who are able to read; and not very bright three year olds at that. Well, very young children are catered for quite adequately by their mothers, as a rule, who tell them such stories as will widen their eyes and then close them in a happy sleep. But mercifully there are still some writers today who write for the joy of telling such a story as will delight all who read it. Although they are published as writers for the young, they are indeed writers for us all, and the adult who can take no pleasure in their work is in a sad way.

So here, then, is a book, not just for the twelve year old, but for the family. Although most of the authors who have contributed are among the best and most famous of writers published for the young, they are all expert storytellers whose work would stand high in any company. Also among the contributors there are some three or four whose work has been chiefly adult. To my mind they all stand on the same level and differences are in tone of voice rather than complications of thought.

So now to *Baker's Dozen* itself. To open any book of essays or short stories by many authors is like entering a room of strangers. Some are talkative and friendly and fascinating from the very beginning; others are more reserved and take a little time to get to know. It is impossible to like them all at once; but it is very unlikely not to find a few friends in so varied a company.

Here they are, then; thirteen strangers eager and very well able to please. Open the book and meet them; and may you find thirteen friends.

Joan Aiken is one of those very rare authors who is published both as an adult writer and juvenile. She writes first-rate detective stories and first-rate humorous fantasies, such as *Black hearts in Battersea* and *The Wolves of Willoughby Chase* set in a strange historical period of her own invention.

Edward Blishen, famous in the field of education, has written two marvellous books about his experiences in a North London School; *The Roaring Boys*, and *This Right Soft Lot*. Both are as true and funny as any books I know about school.

If Helen Cresswell's story doesn't bring a smile to your lips, I am sorry for you. Though *The Piemakers* is her most famous book, her others are equally good and all are distinguished by rich comic invention and a style that anyone might envy.

Alan Garner is as strange and unpredictable as the tale he's chosen to tell. Folk lore is his passion and the use he makes of it in his novels is deeply impressive. *The Owl Service* and *Elidor* are perhaps his most successful books, but anything with his name to it is well worth the reading. His power of telling a story is very considerable.

Tom Hutchinson is not a novelist. He is a critic and a journalist of real distinction; but to my mind his best work is to be found in a series of interviews with the stars and would-be stars of show business. Though never cruel, these interviews are as sharp as a scalpel in revealing the human being under the sequins. It is such an interview that I asked him to write . . . an imaginary interview with such a performer as he has met and talked to many, many times.

The reputation of William Mayne stands very high indeed; and the very opening of his story tells the reader why. There is such distinction in everything he writes, such a marvellous use of words and so subtle a sense of humour that one is amazed by the amount he has written without his standards faltering. Among a legion of brilliant books *Earthfasts* and *Sand* spring most readily to mind, together with *A Swarm in May* as being richest of the rich.

Iona McGregor is a new writer—and as fresh as a daisy. Her novels of Eighteenth Century Edinburgh are as sharp and witty as one could wish. Her characters live and talk straight off the printed page. Read *An Edinburgh Reel* or *The Burning Hill* and you'll see what I mean.

Philip Oakes is a very eminent novelist, poet and critic who, to my knowledge has never thought of writing particularly for the young. But read his story and see what you've been missing if you ever imagined that good writers are dull to read.

Jill Paton-Walsh, like Alan Garner, is deeply interested in ancient things. But it is history rather than fantasy that absorbs her. She writes of the Sagas of the Vikings—and she writes as the Vikings themselves wrote or told their adventures. The strength and power of her work is truly remarkable; and she possesses the rarest gift of the historical novelist which is to bring an ancient time convincingly to life; and not only ancient times: *Fireweed* is a first-rate novel about the blitz.

Although it would be impossible to arrange all these distinguished authors in order of merit, if one had to do so I don't think there'd be any doubt that Philippa Pearce would be high in the list. *Tom's Midnight Garden* is perhaps the most perfect book written for the young in this generation. Nor is that one book all. *A Dog So Small* and *The Children of the House* are both marked by the same extraordinary talent.

Like Philippa Pearce, Catherine Storr has written one book that lives and lingers in the mind long after one had read it. *Marianne Dreams* is one of those strange rare fantasies that catches the heart and holds it. Her story, like all her work and, indeed, like herself, is graceful, humorous and perceptive and is informed by a deep understanding of the human heart.

Last, but only because his name begins with a 'T' is John Rowe Townsend. It is said we live in a Golden Age of Children's Books; and John Rowe Townsend's work is one of the reasons why. *Gumble's Yard*, *Widdershins' Crescent* and *Pirate's Island* are household names in those houses where the best in modern storytelling is read and treasured. More recently, *The Intruder* and *Goodnight, Prof., Love*, have startled and delighted even his sternest critics into admitting that here at last is a writer we can all enjoy. But here he has written, not a story, but an account of his own career as a journalist on that best of all papers: *The Guardian*.

Leon Garfield

THE ELM STREET LOT AND THE RED SPORTS CAR

by Philippa Pearce

At the end of Elm Street there stood an elm-tree—once upon a time; now just a tree-stump. The stump is the meeting-place of the Elm Street lot. Their lot always hangs together: there may be argument round the old stump, but not often quarrelling. Never—or almost never—fighting.

The last time there was a fight, it was between Sim Tolland and Johnny Bates; and it was about the peace and quiet of Elm Street. Elm Street usually *is* very quiet, especially in the evening; but Di Bates and Old Father Time make two exceptions to that.

Di Bates, whose full name is Diana Marilyn Bates, is a lot older than Johnny and Kitty, and the prettiest girl in Elm Street and for miles round. She's always being taken out in the evening, to dances and cinemas and for moonlight walks. At first it was Sim Tolland's big brother, Bert, who took her; and that was peaceful for everybody. They'd stroll back in the evening to Elm Street from wherever it was; Bert would see Di to her front-door; then he'd walk on to his own.

But Di threw Bert Tolland over for a boy with a motor-bike, and—Di riding pillion—they'd come roaring back late in the evening from wherever it was, and then the bike would go roaring off again. Then just when poor Bert Tolland had saved up to buy an old second-hand car, Di Bates threw the motor-cyclist over for a boy with a smart red sports car, and they'd come roaring back from wherever it was, and there'd be a lot of door-slamming at midnight before Red Sports Car roared off again. Altogether Di Bates's boy-friends were a trial to the sleepers of Elm Street.

And then there was the Tollands' cat. Perhaps once, long ago he had been a kitten, called Fluffy or Tibs or something like that; but now he was just called Old Father Time. He was old, old; and he had lost an eye, and limped badly. And Old Father Time's habit every so often was to saunter slowly down Elm Street at about midnight, yowling.

The night before the fight at the tree-stump, Old Father Time was doing this as usual, and Mr. Crackenthorpe had troubled to get out of bed and open a front window and throw a boot—with shocking aim. He had hit a street lamp, breaking the glass. All that he had then said about Old Father Time had been overheard quite clearly by Mrs. Bates, who was sitting up in bed waiting for Di to get home. And she had told most of it to Mr. Bates, over breakfast, and so Johnny and Kitty Bates knew it and could tell the rest of the Elm Street lot later, round the tree-stump.

Kitty Bates said: 'Old Cracky finished up by shouting at the top of his voice that that diseased old rag-bag of a tom-cat should be put down.'

'And if your dad wouldn't do it, Sim' said Johnny Bates, 'then old Cracky himself would go round to the animal-cruelty people and ask them to do it.'

Sim Tolland was annoyed. 'Perhaps you don't know what my dad said to old Cracky when he came puffing round this morning?'

'Go on,' said Johnny.

'He said that if anyone needed putting down it was old Cracky, and he'd ask the Council to do it, and to send the Refuse Disposal to clear up afterwards.'

Everyone at the tree-stump liked that; but Sim wasn't content,

perhaps because he knew—and he knew that Johnny Bates knew—about Bert's being thrown over by Di. He went on: 'And then my dad said that if Cracky really objected to noise at night, why hadn't he the guts to throw his other boot at that red sports car with no silencer that brings your sister home every night; and give up persecuting poor old defenceless cats?'

'Who says that sports car hasn't a silencer?' said Johnny.

'I do,' said Sim.

But, of course, they weren't quarrelling about a car-silencer. The next remark brought them a bit nearer to what they *were* quarrelling about.

'Anyway,' said Johnny, 'that sports car really goes, which is more than can be said for your brother's poor old second hand thing living under its plastic sheet.'

That was when Sim Tolland went for Johnny Bates, and Johnny Bates fought back.

You might have thought the fight would have been over in half a minute or so because Sim is older and bigger and stronger than Johnny; but it wasn't, and that was because of Kitty Bates. She'd been standing by, listening, with the rest of the Elm Street lot, and now she went right in to help Johnny, fighting like a demon. She's tough. Sim Tolland—who rather likes her in peacetime—held her right off the ground by her hair, but she just went on biting.

Nobody knows who might have won, because just then Bert Tolland himself turned up, on his way home. Kitty Bates drew off at once; and Bert took a good hold of the other two and pulled them apart to stop them. Then he saw who they were.

'My!' he said, good tempered, if gloomy. 'My, my. I thought you two were always as thick as thieves—and up to as much good. What's made you fall out now? What's up?'

At first neither of them wanted to say, but Bert gave them both a bit of a shake, and then Sim said: 'He was saying things about Old Father Time.'

Bert Tolland laughed; and that annoyed both Sim and Johnny.

Johnny said quickly, 'And *he* was saying things about the sports car that brings Di home.'

Bert Tolland stopped laughing, and frowned.

Sim went on eagerly, 'And *he* said the sports car was better than your car; and *I* was saying—'

Bert Tolland never heard what Sim had said. He was scowling ferociously, and he shook those two boys until the rest of the Elm Street lot heard their teeth clattering in their heads. Then he took Johnny Bates by the scruff of his collar, like a puppy, and set him on the top of the elm street stump; and he took Sim also by the scruff and pushed him ahead of him to the Tollands' house and in through the front door, and then the front door slammed behind them both. And what Bert Tolland said to Sim Tolland on the other side of that door, nobody knows.

And that was the end of the fighting, but not of the story.

That night Red Sports Car brought Di Bates home as usual, and that night, as usual, Old Father Time decided to take his stroll down Elm Street. And as Red Sports Car was roaring off again from the Bates's house, it met Old Father Time in the middle of the street; the car screeched its brakes for as long as it takes to run over and kill a cat, and then it roared on and away, and there was poor Old Father Time lying dead in the middle of the road.

People didn't rush out of their houses at the noise, as they would have done in the daytime. But two people in Elm Street, in two different houses, had been listening particularly for the sound of the red sports car: one of them was Di Bates, of course, just home, still dressed up from her evening out; and the other was Bert Tolland, insomniac.

Within half a minute of the screeching of brakes Di Bates had reopened their front door to see what had happened, and within another half minute Bert Tolland was peering out, too. What he saw was Di Bates now standing in the middle of Elm Street, looking down—he couldn't see what she was looking at—and something about the way she stood there made him want to rush out to her. But it was weeks since Di Bates and Bert Tolland had as much as said good-day to each other; so Bert Tolland rushed back into the house instead and up to Sim's room and began pulling him out of bed and putting shoes on him and a coat round him.

'What—what on earth is it?' said Sim sleepily.

'Shut up—shut up! Get up and get out into the street and ask Di Bates what's the matter. And if anything is the matter, call me and I'll come.'

Sim was now wide awake, but just as confused as if he weren't.

'But, Bert, —' he began.

'Do me this favour,' said Bert, 'and I'll do anything for you—anything. Go and make sure that Di Bates is all right; and I'll give you the moon. I promise.'

Bert's promise somehow cleared Sim's head; but he wanted to be quite sure. 'Suppose I wanted to go with you in the first real trip in the car?'

'Yes, yes.'

'And me, not you, to decide which is the first real trip?'

'Yes, yes, *yes*. Only *go*.'

So Sim went, bouncing out of the house for joy at the thought of Bert's promise. And there was Di Bates still in the middle of Elm Street, but kneeling now, and when Sim saw what she was kneeling by—poor Old Father Time's body—all the bounce went out of Sim.

'Oh!' he said. He stood still as a statue of marble. Bert Tolland, peering through the crack of their front door, saw Di Bates get up and put her arm round him.

'He must have been killed at once,' Di said to Sim. 'The car must have gone right over him.'

'He never even stopped,' said Sim. He meant the driver, whose name you will not be told, for a reason that comes later.

'He can't have realized what he'd done,' said Di.

Sim moved. He began to stoop: 'I'll take him.'

'Wait.' Di stripped off a smart new cardigan, and they wrapped Old Father Time in it. Then Sim carried him back to the Tolland's house, where Bert met him at the door, and Bert carried the bundle into the back garden, where Old Father Time had often taken the sun or a sparrow as the case might be.

Then and there, by moonlight, they buried him, so that their mother would not see him in the morning—although she and Mr. Bates would have to be told, of course. They did not bury him in Di's cardigan, but Sim fetched a piece of clean sacking, and Bert dug a hole three spits deep, and so they buried him; and later in the year Sim planted forget-me-nots over him.

The next morning Sim, pale from grieving and lack of sleep, told their parents. Mrs. Tolland was terribly upset, and cried, as had been expected. Mr. Tolland, to comfort her and Sim, said that, after all, Old Father Time had been getting on: he was bound to go some day.

'But not run over by a car,' said Sim.

'By a car that didn't trouble to stop,' said Bert.

'I expect that young fellow of Di Bates's didn't realize,' said Mr. Tolland.

'Didn't realize—nothing!' said Bert.

When she felt better, Mrs. Tolland washed Di's cardigan and was going to take it back to her when Bert said: 'I'll take it—this evening.'

By that evening, of course, the whole of Elm Street had heard of the death, and a good many were wondering what was going to happen next. In spite of the lateness of the hour, there were quite a few of the Elm Street lot gathered at the tree-stump to see the red sports car come as usual to pick Di Bates up. Sim was all for tackling the driver at once, but Bert said, 'Wait.'

He came. He drove his red sports car with the usual roar and rattle up to the Bates's house, and at once the front door opened and there was Di Bates, all dressed up for the dance they were going to.

"Hello!" said red sports car. 'Ready?'

'Yes.' But she hesitated. 'Last night, when you were driving away, the car hit something.'

'Hit something?'

'A cat.'

'Did it?'

'Didn't you know?'

'Well, now you mention it. . . . In fact, I thought I'd probably killed the thing.'

Di stared for a long minute, and then—like Bert Tolland earlier—she said, 'Wait.'

She went indoors and came out again with her mother's shopping basket. From this she began to take a number of things in a hurry: a little bottle of scent, a box of scented soap, an embroidered handkerchief, bathsalts—all the things that red sports car had ever given her. One by one, but quite fast, she threw them at him or on the ground near him. There were even two bunches of wet-stemmed flowers and a box of chocolates, half eaten. The Elm Street lot crawled over the ground afterwards and collected everything of use, so they knew.

At the very end, so that there could be no mistake, Di Bates slapped his face. Then she went indoors, and Red Sports Car called some names after her and then drove off at a really frightful speed, still shouting. And this is why it wasn't worth telling you his proper name, for he was never, never seen in Elm Street again.

That was the moment that Bert Tolland chose for the returning of Di Bates's cardigan. Mrs. Bates, who answered the door to him, said that Di was really in no fit state to see anybody; but Bert just sidled in, and Mrs. Bates had to shut the door behind him, and that was that.

For the rest of that week Di Bates didn't go out in the evening at all; but Bert Tolland became cheerful again. He took the plastic cover off his old car and began tinkering with it to make it go properly. He wanted it right for an afternoon trip on Saturday, he said.

'Where to?' Sim asked.

'Right into the country,' Bert said blithely. 'Di says she'll come. To Borden Woods and then to Borden Bridge, where you can hire a boat.'

'I'll come too,' said Sim.

'You're joking,' said Bert, grinning. Then he stopped grinning, as he remembered his midnight promise: 'No, you're not.'

Sim wasn't joking. He was choosing to go on this first long car trip, when Bert happened to be taking Di. Nothing Bert could say would budge him.

Bert was very upset; but Di Bates—for a wonder—was not. She laughed a lot, and said that if Sim were coming, then it would be just as well if Kitty and Johnny came too. So they all went.

Saturday was fine, and the old car went like a bird. They got to Borden Woods, but not to the river. In the woods Kitty and Johnny and Sim stuck together, but they got separated from the other two, somehow. They were looking for each other, on and off, for hours on end.

When at last they did find each other, it was time to go home. Bert and Di were not as cross as might have been expected. Bert said he had enjoyed the afternoon, in spite of everything; and Di Bates laughed a lot.

THE FLYING CHILDER
by Alan Garner

Translated from the original Lincolnshire

I'm scare sure if I can tell you it all right, but I guess I mind it as it was told to me. Let's see, now.

There was once a chap as was great for the womenfolk, and couldn't keep out of their way if he tried ever so. The very sight of a petticoat half a mile off on the road would call him for to follow it.

Now one day, as it might be, he came ker-bang round a corner, and there was a ramping maid, sitting her lone, and washing herself; and the fond chap was all out of his wits to want. And the upshot of it was, he swore he would wed her if she would come home with him. And she said:

'I'll come, and welcome,' says she, 'but you must swear as you'll wed me.'

'I will,' says he, 'I swear it!'—and thought to himself, 'Over the left shoulder, that!'

'You must wed me in church,' says she.

'I will!' says he. 'If ever I put foot in,' he thought to himself.

'And if you don't, what shall I forspell you?' says she.

'Lawks,' says he, for he was feared of being forspelled, which is main mischancy, you see; 'don't you overlook me, don't you! If I don't wed you, may the worms eat me'—(They're bound for to do it, anyway, thinks he to himself)—'and the children have wings and fly away.' (And no great matter if they do.)

But the maid didn't know as he was thinking, and she went with him. And by and by they came to a church.

'You can wed me here-by,' says she, tweaking his arm.

'No,' said he, 'the parson's a-hunting.'

So they went on a bit further, and came to another church.

'Well, here-by?' says she.

'No,' says he. 'Parson's none sober enough, and the clerk's drunk.'

'Well!' says she. 'May be they will can wed us, for all they're in liquor.'

'Houts!' says he, and gives her a kick.

So on they went again, and by and by they met with a tailor-man, and he says, says he:

'Where's your master?'

'Oh, down by,' says the old feller.

So on they went, while they came to a bit cottage by the lane side, and they knocked and kicked at the door till it shook, but never a word came from innard. So they walked right in, and there was an old man lying sleeping and snoring on his bed.

Well, the young chap keckt about him for summat handy, and saw an axe, so he upped with it and brained the old feller, and chopped his feet and hands off him. And then he set to and cleaned the place, and thrung the corp out of the window, and laid the fire in the hearth, while all was smart and natty.

Then they lived there, and had some childer.

And by and by, kecking over his shoulder, the chap saw a wise woman stealing the corp away with her.

'I'll bury him for you,' says the wise woman.

'No you won't,' says he; 'I can do it better my lone.'

'Take your way, fool,' says she, 'But give me the axe, then, instead of the corp.'

'No I won't,' says he. 'I might want her again.'

'Hi!' says the wise woman. 'None give, none have; red hand and lying lips!'

And she went away, muttering, and twisting her fingers.

So the chap buried the corp, but lest he forget where it was, he left one arm sticking out of the ground, and the feet and hands he chucked to the pigs, and says he to the girl:

'I'll go and snare a cony. See you keep to the house.' And off he went.

The girl diddle-daddled about, and presently the pigs began squealing as if they were killed.

'And oh!' says the girl, 'what's amiss with them, for so to squeal?'

And the dead feet upped and cried, 'We be amiss. Us'll trample the pigs till you bury us!'

So she took the feet and put them in the earth.

And by and by the pigs lay down and died.

'Oh! oh!' says the girl. 'What be the matter with them for so to die?'

And the dead hands upped and cried, 'We be the matter. We's choked them!'

So she went and buried them, too.

And by and by she heard summat a-calling, and a-calling on her, and she went for to see what it wanted.

'Who be a-calling?' says she.

'You've put us wrong!' says the feet and hands.

'We be feeling, and we be creeping, and we can't find the rest of us anywheres. Put us by the old man, where his arms sticks out of the ground, or we'll tickle with fingers and tread you with toes, till you lose your wits.'

So she dug them up, and put them by the old man.

And by and by the young chap came back, and called for his dinner.

'Where's the childer?' says he.

'Gathering berries,' says she.

'Berries in Spring?' says he; and kept on with his eating. But when night came, and they weren't home:

'Where's the childer?' says he.

'Gone a-fishing,' says she.

'Ay,' says he, 'and the babby, too?'

And came the morning, he shook the girl up sudden, and bawled in her ears:

'Where's the childer?'

'Ooh!' says she in a hurry, 'flown away, the children have!'

'They have?' says he. 'Then you will can go after them!'

And he upped with the axe and chopped her in pieces, and shoved the bits under the bed.

Well, by and by, the childer came flying back, and keckt about for their mother, but they saw nowt.

'Where's mother?' they says to the chap.

'Gone to buy bacon,' says he, feeling uneasy.

'Bacon?' says they. 'And with flitches hanging ready?'

And presently they came again, and says:

'Where's mother now?'

'Gone to seek you,' says he, shaking under the bedclothes.

'Ay?' says they. 'And we be here!'

And before he could get out of bed they came all round him, and pointed at him with their fingers.

'Where's mother to-now?'

'Ooh!' he squealed. 'Under the bed!' And he put his head under the blanket.

The children pulled out the bits, and fell to weeping and wailing as they pieced her together. And the chap, he went for to creep to the door and get away, but they caught him, and took the axe and chopped him up like the girl, and left him lying whiles they went away, gratting.

As soon as he was sure he was dead, the chap got up and shook himself—and there was the girl! She was standing waiting for him, with long claws out, and teeth gibbering, and eyes blazing like a green cat going to spring. And naturally the chap was feared, and he runned, and runned, and runned, so as to get away; but she runned after, with her long claws straight out, till he could feel her tickling the back of his neck, and straining with the longing to choke him. And he called out to the thunder:

'Strike me dead!'

But the thunder wouldn't, for he was dead already.

And he runned to the fire and begged:

'Burn me up!'

But the fire wouldn't, for the chill of death put it out.

And he thrung himself in the water and says:

'Drown me blue!'

But the water wouldn't, for the death-colour was coming in his face already.

And he took the axe and tried to cut his throat, but the axe wouldn't.

And to last, he thrung himself into the ground, and called for the worms to eat him, so as he could rest in his grave and be quit of the woman.

But by and by up crept a great worm, and a strange and great thing it was, with the girl's head on the end of its long slimy body, and it crept up beside him and round about, and over him, while it drove away all the other worms, and then it set to, to eat him itself.

'Ooh, eat me quick, eat me quick!' he squeals.

'Steady, now,' says the worm. 'Good food's worth the meal time.

You hold still, and let me enjoy myself.'

"Eat me quick, eat me quick!' says he.

'Don't you haste me, I tell you,' says the worm.

'I's getting on fine. You're near gone now.' And it smacked its lips with the goodness of it.

'Quick!' he whispit again.

'Whist, you're an unpatient chap,' said the worm.

And it swalled the last bit, and the lad was all gone, and had got away from the girl to last.

And that's all.

HOPE
by Joan Aiken

It was on a clear, frosty November evening, not many years ago, that Doctor Jane Smith, having occasion to visit a patient in the part of London known as Rumbury Town, was suddenly overtaken by the impulse to call on an old teacher of hers, a Miss Lestrange, who had a bedsitting-room on the edge of that district, where she earned a meagre living by giving lessons on the harp.

Rumbury Town is a curious region of London. Not far from the big stations, adjacent to Islington, beyond, or anyway defying the jurisdiction of smokeless fuel legislation, it lies enfolded generally in an industrial dusk of its own. The factories of Rumbury Town are not large, and their products are eccentric—artificial grass for butchers' windows, metal bed-winches, false teeth for sheep, slimmers' biscuits made from woodpulp, catnip mice, plastic Christmas-tree decorations—these are a random sample of its exports. But the small gaunt chimneys, leaning from the factories at various precarious angles, belch black smoke as vigorously as any modern electric power station, and so do those of the houses, like rows of organ-stops, along the ill-lit, dour little terraced streets that lead up in the direction of Rumbury Waste, the ragged strip of tree-grown land fringing Rumbury Town on its eastern edge.

Rumbury Waste is a savage place enough, on no account to be visited after dark, but many a police officer would agree that the centre of Rumbury Town itself is far more of a hostile wilderness, by far more dangerous. Here lies an area of mixed factory, business premises, and wholesale market, interspersed with a few lanes of private dwellings and some dingy little shopping precincts; seamed by narrow alleys and shortcuts; a real maze where, it is said, only those born in Rumbury Town or who have spent at least forty years within earshot of the bells of St. Griswold's Rumbury, can ever hope to find their way.

So cold and clear was this particular evening, however, that even the smoke from the Rumbury chimneys had dwindled to a slaty wisp against the sky's duck-egg green; so little wind was there that in the derelict corners of factory lots where goldenrod and willowherb cloaked piles of rubble, the withered leaves and feathery seeds drifted straight and unswerving to ground.

Engines and presses in the factories had ceased their clanging and thudding; workers had gone home; in the centre of Rumbury Town the only sound to be heard was the distant, muted roar of London; and a nearer surge of pop music, sizzle of fish frying, and shouts of children from the few inhabited streets.

Dr. Smith parked her car in one of these, locked it carefully, and went in search of her friend, Miss January Lestrange.

Rumbury Town seemed a curious environment for a spinster who taught the harp. And Miss Lestrange was a real spinster of the old-fashioned kind; she walked very slowly, with small, precise steps; she wore tight, pointed button boots, very shiny, which ended half-way up her calf, and long serge skirts, trimmed with rows of braid, which hung down over the boots; it was pure chance that Miss Lestrange's style of dressing was now once more the height of fashion, and a circumstance that she would certainly not have noticed; had she done so she might have been mildly irritated. Her grey hair was smoothly drawn back into a bun, and she wore pince-nez; all the children of Rumbury Town wondered how she managed to make them balance on her nose. Miss Lestrange kept herself to herself and never troubled her neighbours; many of them, if they had thought about it, would not have been surprised to be told that she was a thin, grey old ghost, occasionally to be seen gliding out on her small shopping errands. And the children, though they were not exactly frightened of her, never chalked on her door, or threw ice-lolly sticks after her, or sang rude rhymes about her, as they did about most other adults in the neighbourhood. Miss Lestrange, however, was no ghost, and although she had lived within sound of St. Griswold's bells for forty years, was not a born citizen of the district; she still did not venture into the twilit heart of Rumbury Town.

'Why *do* you live here?' Dr. Smith asked, when she had knocked on the faded blue door with its postcard: J. Lestrange, Harp Tuition, and had been admitted, passing on his way out a small frantic-looking boy with a music-case under his arm.

'It amazes me the way some of them keep on coming,' murmured Miss Lestrange, zipping its case over the harp, which was as tall, gaunt, and worn-looking as she herself. 'I've told them and told them that you don't get a first-rate harpist once in a generation, but they all think they have the seed of it in them.'

'What about that boy? Is he any good?'

Miss Lestrange shrugged.

'He's the same as the rest. I don't hold false hopes and sweet promises. I send him away at the end of the lesson utterly despondent, limp as rhubarb, but by next time he's always plucked up heart again and thinks he'll be a second David—Well, Jane, it is nice to see you. What brings you here?'

'Suppose I said that *I* wanted some more lessons?' Dr. Smith asked with a small, grim smile.

'I should tell you what I told your parents: it would be a waste of their money, my time, and yours, to teach you for another five minutes.'

'And they at least believed you. So I went away and trained for a doctor.'

'And have turned into a good one, from what I hear.' Miss Lestrange nodded at her ex-pupil affectionately. 'I hope you will stay and take your evening meal with me and tell me about your work.'

But her glance strayed a little doubtfully to the screened

corner of the room where she cooked over a methylated-spirit lamp; she had been about to brew herself a nourishing, or at least vitamin-rich soup, made from hot water, parsley, grown in her window-box, and salt.

'No, no. I came to invite you out. I have to pay one call on a patient not far from here, and then I thought we'd go to the Chinese Restaurant at the corner of Inkermann Street. Put on your coat and let's be off.'

Miss Lestrange was always businesslike.

'Well, that would certainly be a more enjoyable meal than the one I could have offered you,' she said, put on her coat, and a black hat which had the shape though not the festive air of a vol-au-vent, and ushered out her visitor, locking the door behind them.

The little grimy street was silent and watchful. Half a dozen children stared, to see Miss Lestrange setting out at such an unwonted time of day, in such an unwonted manner, in a car, with a friend.

Dr. Smith reverted to her first, unanswered question.

'Why *do* you live here?'

'The rents are very low, Miss Lestrange said mildly. 'Five pounds a year for my room.'

'But in a better part you might get more pupils—brighter ones . . .'

'The world is not that full of gifted harpists,' Miss Lestrange said drily. And the neighbourhood suits me.'

'You have friends here?'

'Once I did. One friend. We have not seen each other for some time. But as one grows older,' Miss Lestrange said calmly, 'one requires fewer friends.'

Reflecting that it would be difficult to have fewer friends than *one*, Dr. Smith brought her car to a halt by a large, grim tenement with a dozen arched entrances. The road that passed it was an old, wide, cobbled one, and on the opposite side began the cluttered, dusky jumble of piled-up factory, warehouse, shed, storehouse, office, factory, and lumber-yard that like a great human badger-warren covered the heart of Rumbury Town.

'My patient lives just through here; I shan't be long.'

'Who is your patient?' inquired Miss Lestrange, as the doctor turned to lift her black case from the rear seat of the car.

'Well, as a matter of fact he's quite well-known—the writer Tom Rampisham. Why, like you, he chooses to live in this god-forsaken spot I don't know, but here he's lived for goodness knows how many years. He has a ground-floor flat in that gloomy block.'

'Tom Rampisham,' Miss Lestrange said musingly. 'It is some time since he did one of his broadcasts. What's his trouble?'

'Heart. Well, I probably shan't be more than a few minutes. But here's a spare car-key in case you want to stroll about.'

It looked an uncompromising area for a stroll. But when Dr. Smith's few minutes lengthened to ten, and then to fifteen, Miss Lestrange, who seemed restless and disinclined to sit still, even after a long day's work, got out of the car, locked it, and stood irresolutely on the pavement.

For a moment she stared at the large forbidding block into which the doctor had vanished. Then, with decision, she turned her back on it and struck off briskly across the road. Almost immediately opposite the car was a little opening in the clifflike façade of warehouses, one of those narrow lanes which the denizens of Rumbury Town call *hackets*, which led inwards, with many angles and windings and sudden changes of direction, towards the heart of the maze.

Along this alley Miss Lestrange rapidly walked. It seemed as if she walked *from* rather than *to* anything in particular; her head was bent, her eyes fixed on the greasy cobbles, she ignored the entrances with their mysterious signs: Wishaw, Flock Sprayers; Saloop, Ear Piercing Specialists; Ample Tops; The Cake Candle Co; Madame Simkins, Feathers; Sugg, Ganister Maker and Refractory Materials Manufacturer; Toppling Seashell Merchants; Shawl, String, and Sheepskin Co; Willow Specialists and Wood Wool Packers. One and all, she passed them without a glance, even the Shawl, String, and Sheepskin office which was in fact the source of her new harp-strings when the old ones had snapped under the inexpert fingers of the youth of Rumbury Town.

Miss Lestrange walked fast, talking to herself, as elderly people do who lead solitary lives.

'If he were ill he might ask for me,' she muttered, going past Gay Injectors and Ejectors without sparing a thought to wonder what obscure goods or services their name denoted. 'He once said he might; I remember his saying that if he were taken ill he might get in touch with me; it's queer that I can hardly remember what we quarrelled about, and yet I can remember that.'

The alley took a turn, widened, and led her into a melancholy little area of street market: crockery stalls, cheap clothing stalls, vegetable stalls, second-hand book and junk stalls. The traders were just closing up for the night, piling their unsold wares—of which there seemed a great many—back into cartons; the way was impeded by boxes of rubbish, and slippery with squashed vegetables, but Miss Lestrange stepped briskly round and over these obstacles without appearing to notice them.

'What did we quarrel about, all that long time ago?' she mused, neatly by-passing a pram loaded with dusty tins of furniture polish and stepping over a crate labelled Supershine Wholesale: We Promise Dazzling Results. 'It was something to do with his poetry, was it?'

The lane narrowed again and she went on between great overhanging cliffs of blackened brick, frowning a little, over her pince-nez, as she tried to summon up a young, lively, impatient face. What had he looked like, exactly? At one time she had known his face by heart—better than her own for Miss Lestrange had never been one to spend much time gazing at herself in mirrors. Noticeable cheekbones; a lock of hair that always fell forward; that was all she could remember.

We Promise Dazzling Results.

'I don't *know* anything about poetry, Tom. How can I say if it's good or bad?'

'You've got an *opinion*, haven't you, girl? You can say what you *think*?'

'You don't really want me to say what I think. You just want me to praise them.'

'Damn it, that's not true, January. January! he said bitterly. 'There never was a more appropriate bit of classification. If ever anybody was ice-cold, frozen hard, ungenerous, utterly unwilling to give an inch, it's you!'

'*That's* not true!' she had wanted to cry. 'It's just that I can't praise what I don't understand, I won't make pretty speeches just to encourage. How can I tell about your poetry? How can I say if I don't know? It wouldn't be right.'

But he had already stuffed the disputed poems into an old black satchel and gone striding off; that was the last time she had seen him.

She passed a cafe with an inscription in what looked like white grease on its window-glass: Sausages, potatoes, onions, peas; frying now, always frying. Why not try our fry?

A staggeringly strong, hot waft of sausage and onion came from the open door; inside were boys with tiny heads, tiny eyes, and huge feet in huge boots; as she hurried by Miss Lestrange felt their eyes investigating her and then deciding that she was not worth the trouble. The hot smell of food made her feel sick and reminded her that she was trembling with hunger; for her lunch at midday she had eaten half a hardboiled egg, for her breakfast a cup of milkless tea.

'I suppose I shall have to put my fees up,' she thought, frowning again.

A shrill whistle, with something familiar about it, disturbed her train of thought, and she glanced ahead. It was the tune, not the whistle, that was familiar: in a moment she identified it as a tune she had written herself, an easy tune for beginners on the harp; she had called it *Snowdrops*.

And rollerskating heedlessly in her direction, whistling it shrilly, but in tune, came the boy to whom she had just finished giving a lesson earlier that evening when Dr. Smith arrived.

Their surprise at meeting was equal. He had almost run into her; he skidded to a jerky stop, braking himself with a hand on the alley wall.

'Miss Lestrange! Coo, *you're* a long way from home, aren't you? You lost your way?'

'Good evening, David. No, I have not lost my way,' Miss Lestrange replied briskly. 'I am simply taking a walk.' What is there surprising in that? her tone expressed.

David looked startled; then he gave her a teasing, disbelieving grin, which made his crooked eyebrows shoot off round the corners of his face. She had never noticed this trick before; but then of course in his lessons he never *did* grin; he was always sweatingly anxious and subdued.

'*I* don't believe you're just out for a walk; I think you're after that there buried treasure!'

'Buried treasure? What buried treasure, pray?'

'Why, the treasure they say's buried somewhere under the middle of Rumbury Town. That's what *you*'re after! But you won't find it! They say the old Devil's keeping an eye on it for himself. If I were you, Miss Lestrange, I'd turn back before you *do* get lost!'

'I shall do no such thing,' Miss Lestrange said firmly, and she went on her way, and David went skating zigzag on *his* way, whistling again the little tune, Snowdrops—'Mi,re,doh, Snowdrops in the snow . . .'

But Miss Lestrange did turn and look once after David, slightly puzzled. He was so different, so much livelier and more sure of himself than during her lessons; he had quite surprised her.

But as for getting lost—what nonsense.

Nevertheless, in a couple of minutes, without being aware of it, Miss Lestrange did lose herself. She came to a point where five alleys met at an open space shaped like a star, chose one at random, walked a fair way along it, came to another similar intersection, and chose again. Rumbury Town folded itself round her. The green sky overhead was turning to navy-blue.

And all around her was dark, too; like the crater of an extinct volcano. An occasional orange streetlight dimly illuminated the alleyway. Not a sound was to be heard. It was a dead world.

Suddenly Miss Lestrange felt uneasy. Her thoughts flew to the professional visit taking place behind her, from the vision of which she had so determinedly started away. Jane must have left him by now. Probably in the car, wondering where I've got to. I had better turn back.

She turned back. And came to the first star-shaped conjunctions of lanes.

'Which was mine?' She stood wondering. All four openings facing her looked blank, like shut drawers; she could find no recognisable feature in any of them. The names were just visible: Lambskin Alley, New Year Way, Peridot Lane, Hell Passage; none of them did she consciously remember seeing before.

'I'd surely have noticed New Year Lane,' she thought, and so chose Hell Passage—not that it looked any more familiar than the rest. What may have caught her unwitting ear was the faint thrum and throb of music, somewhere far away in that direction; as she proceeded along the narrow passage the sound became steadily more identifiable as music, though Miss Lestrange could not put a name to the actual *tune*; but then the world of pop music was unfamiliar territory to her. At least, though, music meant people, and inhabited regions; just for a minute or two, back there, although she would not have admitted it to anybody, Miss Lestrange had felt a stirring of panic at the vacuum of silence all round her.

On she went; crossed another star-shaped conjunction of alleys and, by the light of one high-up orange sodium tube, hung where the youth of Rumbury Town were unlikely to be able to break it by throwing bottles, saw that Hell Passage still continued, bisecting the angle between Sky Peals Lane and Whalebone Way.

'Curious names they have hereabouts; it must be a very old quarter. I shall look up the names on the map if—when I get home. *Did* I come this way?' Miss Lestrange asked herself; another surge of anxiety and alarm swept over her as she passed the closed premises of the Prong, Thong, and Trident Company—surely she would have noticed *that* on the way along?

But the music was much louder now; at least, soon, she must encounter somebody whom she could ask.

Then, without any question, she knew that she was lost. For Hell Passage came to a stop—or rather, it opened into a little cul-de-sac yard out of which there was no other exit. Miss Lestrange could see quite plainly that there was no other exit because the yard was illuminated by a fierce, flickering, variable light which came from bundles of tarry rags stuffed into road-menders' tripods and burning vigorously. These were set against the walls. There were about a dozen people in the yard, and Miss Lestrange's first reaction was one of relief.

'It's one of those pop groups,' she thought. 'I've heard it's hard for them, when they're starting, to find places to practise; I suppose if you can't afford to hire a studio, somewhere like this, far off and out of earshot, would be a godsend.'

Somehow the phrase *out of earshot*, though she had used it herself, made her feel uncomfortable; the beat and howl of the music, failing to fight its way out of the narrow court, was so tremendous, that it gave her a slight chill to think what a long way she must be from any residential streets, for people not to have complained about it.

She glanced again at the group; decided not to ask them the way, and turned to go quickly and quietly back. But she was too late; she found somebody standing behind her: an enormously large, tall man, dressed in red velvet trousers and jacket, with a frilled shirt.

'Hey now, you're not thinking of *leaving*, are you—when you just got here?' His voice was a genial roar, easily heard even above the boom of the music, but there was a jeering note under its geniality. 'Surely not going to run off without hearing us, were you? Look, boys and girls,' he went on, his voice becoming, without the slightest difficulty, even louder, 'Look who's here! It's Miss Lestrange, Miss January Lestrange; come to give us her critical opinion!'

A wild shout of derisive laughter went up from the group in the court.

'Three cheers for Miss January Lestrange—the hippest harpist in the whole of toe-tapping Rumbury Town!'

They cheered her, on and on, and the tall man led her with grinning mock civility to a seat on an upturned Snowcem tin. The players began tuning their instruments some of which, trumpets and basses, seemed conventional enough, but others were contrivances that Miss Lestrange had never laid eyes on before—zinc washtubs with strings stretched across, large twisted shells, stringed instruments that looked more like weapons—crossbows perhaps—than zithers, strange prehistoric-looking wooden pipes at least six or seven feet long—and surely that was an actual *fire* burning under the kettle-drum?

'January!' the large man boomed, standing just behind the shoulder of Miss Lestrange. 'Now, *there's* a chilly sort of name to give a spirited lady like yourself—a downright cold, miserable kind of a dreary name, isn't it, boys and girls? The worst month of the year!'

'It is not!' snapped Miss Lestrange—but she did wish he would not stand so close, for his presence just out of sight gave her the cold grue—for some odd reason the phrase '*Get thee behind me, Satan*, slipped into her mind—'January means hope, it means looking forward, because the whole year lies ahead.'

But her retort was drowned in the shout from the group of players—'*We*'ll soon warm her up!'

'Happy lot, ain't they?' confided the voice at her back. 'Nick's Nightflowers, we call ourselves—from the location, see?' He pointed up and, by the light of the flaring rags, Miss Lestrange could just read the sign on the wall: Old Nick's Court, E.1. 'And I'm Old Nick, naturally—happy to have you with us tonight, Miss Lestrange.'

She flicked a glance sideways, to see if it would be possible to slip away once they began playing, but to her dismay most of the group were now between her and the entrance, blocking the way; from their grins, it was plain that they knew what she had in mind. And she had never seen such an unattractive crew—'Really,' she thought, 'if they had *tails* they could hardly look less human.'

Old Nick, with his red velvet and ruffles, was about the most normal in appearance and dress, but she cared for him least of all, and unobtrusively edged her Snowcem tin cornerways until at least she had the wall at her back.

'Ready, all? Cool it now—real cool,' called Nick, at which there was a howl of laughter. 'One, two, three—*stomp*!'

The music broke out again. If music it could be called. The sound seemed to push Miss Lestrange's blood backward along her arteries, to flog on her ear-drums, to slam in her lungs, to seize hold of her heart and dash it from side to side.

'I shan't be able to endure it for more than a minute or two,' she thought quite calmly. 'It's devilish, that's what it is—really devilish.'

Just at the point when she had decided she could stand it no longer, half a dozen more figures lounged forward from a shadow at the side of the court, and began to dance. Boys or girls? It was hard to say. They seemed bald, and extraordinarily *thin*—they had white, hollow faces, deepset eyes under bulging foreheads, meaningless grins. 'White satin!' thought Miss Lestrange scornfully. 'And ruffles! What an extraordinarily dated kind of costume—like the pierrot troupes when I was young.'

But at a closer view the satin seemed transparent gauze, or chiffon. 'I've never *seen* anyone so thin—they are like something out of Belsen,' thought Miss Lestrange. 'That one must have had rickets when young—his legs are no more than bones. They must all have had rickets,' she decided.

'D'you like it?' boomed the leader in her ear. It seemed amazing that he could still make his voice heard above the row, but he could.

'Frankly, no,' said Miss Lestrange. 'I never laid eyes on such a spiritless ensemble. They all dance as if they wanted dosing with Parrish's Food and codliver oil.'

'Hear that, gang?' he bawled to the troupe. 'Hear that? The lady doesn't care for your dancing; she thinks you're a lily-livered lot.'

The dancers paused; they turned their bloodless faces toward Miss Lestrange. For a moment she quailed, as tiny lights seemed to burn in the deep eye-sockets, all fixed on her. But then the leader shouted,

'And what's more, *I* think so too! Do it again—and this time, put some guts into it, or it'll be prong, thong, and trident, all right!'

The players redoubled their pace and volume, the dancers broke into a faster shuffle. And the leader, still making himself heard above the maniac noise,

'Hope! Where are you? Come along out, you mangy old tom-cat, you!' And, to the group, '*He*'ll soon tickle you up!'

A dismal and terrified wailing issued from the dancers at these words.

'Hope's a little pet of mine,' confided the leader to Miss Lestrange. 'Makes all the difference when they're a bit sluggish; *you* ought to like him too.'

She distrusted his tone, which seemed to promise some highly unpleasant surprise, and looked round sharply.

A kind of ripple parted the musicians and dancers; at first Miss Lestrange could not see what had caused this, but, even through the music, she thought she could hear cries of pain or terror; then a wave of dancers eddied away from her and a gold-brown animal bounded through, snatching with sabre-teeth at a bony thigh as it passed.

'That's Hope,' said the leader with satisfaction. '*That's* my little tiger-kitten. Isn't he a beauty? Isn't he a ducky-diddums? I powder his fur with pepper and ginger before we start, to put him in a lively mood—and *then* doesn't he chase them about if they're a bit mopish!'

Hope certainly had a galvanizing effect upon the dancers; as he slunk and bounded among them, their leaps and gyrations had the frenzy of a tarantella; sometimes he turned and made a sudden snarling foray among the musicians, which produced a wild flurry of extra discords and double drumbeats.

'Here, puss, puss! Nice pussy, then! There's a lady here who'd like to stroke you.'

Hope turned, and silently sprang in their direction, Miss Lestrange had her first good look at him. He was bigger than a leopard, a brownish-ginger colour all over, with long, angrily switching tail; his fangs glistened white-gold in the fiery light, his eyes blazed like carbuncles; he came towards Miss Lestrange slowly, stalking with head lowered.

And she put out her right hand, confidently running it over his shoulderblades and along the curving knobbed spine; its bristles undulated under the light pressure. 'There, then!' she cried absently. Hope turned, and rubbed his harsh ruff against her hand; elevated his chin to be scratched; finally sat down beside her and swung the long tail neatly into place over formidable talons.

Miss Lestrange thoughtfully pulled his ears; she had always liked cats.

She turned to the leader again.

'I still don't think much of your dancers. And, to be honest, your music seems to me nothing but a diabolical row!'

Silence followed her words. She felt the dark cavities in their faces trained on her, and forced herself not to shrink.

'However, thank you for playing to me. And now I must be going,' she ended politely.

'Dear me.' The leader's tone was thoughtful. 'That fairly puts us in our place, don't it, boys and girls? You certainly are a free-spoken one, Miss January Lestrange. Come now—I'm sure a nice lady, a died-in-the-wool lady like you, wouldn't want to be too hard on the lads, and *really* upset them. Just before you go—if you *do* go—tell me, don't you think that, in time, if they practise hard enough, they might amount to something?'

'I am absolutely not prepared to make such a statement,' Miss Lestrange said firmly. 'Your kind of music is quite outside my province. And I have never believed in flattery.' A kind of rustle ran through the group; they moved closer.

'Our kind of music ain't her province,' the leader said. 'That's true. Tell you what, Miss Lestrange. *You* shall give *us* a tune. Let's have some of *your* kind of music—eh? That'd be a treat for us, wouldn't it, gang?'

They guffawed, crowding closer and closer; she bit her lip.

'Fetch over the harp!' bawled Nick. 'No one in our ensemble actually plays it,' he explained to Miss Lestrange. 'But we like to have one along always—you never know when someone may turn up who's a harp fancier. Like you. No strings, I'm afraid, but we can fix that, easy.'

A warped, battered, peeling old harp was dumped down before her; it had no strings, but one of the dancers dragged up a coil of what looked like telephone cable and began rapidly stringing it to and fro across the frame.

'Now,' said Nick, 'you shall delight us, Miss Lestrange! And if you *do*, then maybe we'll see about allowing you to leave. Really, you know, we'd hate to part from you.

An expectant silence had fallen: an unpleasant, mocking, triumphant silence.

'I haven't the least intention of playing that ridiculous instrument,' Miss Lestrange said coldly. 'And now, I'm afraid you'll have to excuse me; my friend will be wondering where I've got to. Come, Hope.'

She turned and walked briskly to the entrance of the court; there was no need to push her way, they parted before her. Hope trotted at her side.

Far off, down Hall Passage, could be heard a faint, clear whistle coming her way.

But, once out in the alley, Miss Lestrange tottered, and nearly fell; she was obliged to put a hand against the wall to support herself. Seized with a deep chill and trembling, she was afraid to trust her unsteady legs, and had to wait until the boy David reached her, whistling and zig-zagging along on his roller-skates.

'Coo, Miss Lestrange, I *knew* you'd get lost; and you did, didn't you? Thought I'd better come back and see where you'd got to. You all right?' he said, sharply scrutinising her face.

'Yes, thank you, David. I'm quite all right now. I just went a bit further than I intended. I'm a little tired, that's all.'

She glanced back into Old Nick's Court. It was empty: empty and silent. The flares had gone out.

'Well, come on then, Miss Lestrange, just you follow me and I'll take you back to the other lady's car. You can hold on to my anorak if you like,' he suggested.

'That's all right, thank you David, I can manage now.'

So he skated slowly ahead and she walked after him, and a little way in the rear Hope followed, trotting silently in the shadows.

When they came within view of the car—it took a very short time, really—David said, 'I'll say good night then, Miss Lestrange. See you Thursday.'

'Good night, David, and thank you.' Then she called after him: Practise hard, now!'

'Okay, Miss Lestrange.'

There was an ambulance drawn up behind the car.

'Wait there!' she said to Hope. He sat down in the shadows of the alley-mouth.

As Miss Lestrange crossed the road, the ambulance rolled off. Dr. Smith stood looking after it.

'Sorry to be such a time,' she said. 'That poor man—I'm afraid he's not going to make it.'

'You mean—Tom Rampisham?'

'I shouldn't be surprised if he dies on the way. Oh—excuse me a moment—I'll have to lock up his flat and give the key to the porter.'

Without thinking about it, Miss Lestrange followed her ex-pupil. She walked into the untidy room that she had entered—how long? thirty years ago?—and looked at the table, covered with scrawled sheets of paper.

'I don't know who ought to take charge of this,' Dr. Smith said, frowning. 'I suppose he has a next-of-kin somewhere. Well—I'll worry about that tomorrow. Come along—*you* must be starving and exhausted—let's go.'

Miss Lestrange was looking at the top sheet, at the heading HOPE which was printed in large capitals. Halfway down the page a sentence began.

'*It was on a clear, frosty November evening, not many years ago . . .*'

The words tailed off into a blob of ink.

Dr. Smith led the way out. 'It's terribly late. We can still get a meal at the Chinese place, though,' she was saying. 'And afterwards I'll phone up Rumbury Central and find out how— and find out. I really am sorry to have kept you so long. I hope you weren't frozen and bored.'

'No . . . No. I—I went for a walk.'

Miss Lestrange followed the doctor along the echoing concrete passage. And as she went—'I do hope,' she was thinking, 'Oh, I do *hope* that Hope will still be there.'

HOW TO BEGIN
by John Rowe Townsend

Before I became a full-time author I was in journalism for nearly twenty years. Again and again during that time, young people and their parents used to ask me for advice on entering the profession. Sometimes they still do, although it's more than a year since I left it myself. The advice I always give is the famous advice which was once given by *Punch* 'to those about to marry.' It was: 'Don't.'

This is not because I have anything against journalism or journalists. It is because the first qualification you need for success in journalism is a total refusal to be put off by anything that anybody says. If you *can* be discouraged from entering journalism, you *should* be discouraged. You're not determined enough. The life is not for you.

'Listen,' I tell youngsters. 'Do you realise that journalism is the most competitive profession in the world? That a given amount of talent will probably get you less distance in newspapers than anywhere else? That the newspaper world, unlike business or education, is more likely to shrink than expand? That journalists work twice as hard as most other people, and in spite of that are not very popular with the public?

'And listen again,' I say as I get warmed up. 'Maybe you

fancy yourself as the editor of a national newspaper, or at least a glamorous foreign correspondent. But there are only a handful of editorships of national papers, and not many really good jobs for foreign correspondents. And if you *did* get one of those you'd feel you were on duty all the time.

'What's more,' I say if they're still listening, 'you may not be thinking about it now, but some day most likely you'll want to get married. What will your wife (or husband) think about a partner who keeps all kinds of hours, who doesn't know where he'll be next week, who's forever living the job and working unpaid overtime?'

'I don't know,' they say, 'but I'd still like to try.

So then I tell them about the young friend of mine who wrote around, this very year, asking thirty different editors for a job, and got a negative reply from every one of them. But by this time they think I'm being churlish and pessimistic.

'How and why, then' they ask, 'did *you* get into journalism? What sort of work did you do? Did you like it? Why did you leave?'

To start with, I was one of those people who always wanted to write. At school I was concerned in most of the little magazines that were started (and usually soon stopped). Between school and university I got the editor of a provincial paper to let me come in for a few months and work on 'lineage', which is a system of payment by results. My earnings were very small, and probably the most valuable experience I got was that of doing some of the humblest of all jobs in journalism, such as standing at the church door taking the names of people who attended a funeral, and listing the winners at a local agricultural show. Humble as they are, these jobs are difficult and can easily get you into trouble. Mr. Smith, who went to the funeral, will complain if you get his initials wrong, and will complain still more if you fail to record his presence at all. Mrs. Smith, who won first prize for home-made jam at the show, will be equally incensed if you credit her with third prize for cabbages instead, or mix her up with Mrs. Smythe who was a helper in the tea-tent.

At the university, I joined the student newspaper, and my

previous experience helped me to rise quickly from being a reporter to the position of news editor, then editor. Though I say it myself, it was a good little paper, printed on the presses of the local evening paper, and selling at that time about 5,500 copies of each weekly issue.

I remember writing slashing editorials, telling the authorities how a university should be run (they'd been doing it for about 600 years, but we all felt we could teach them a thing or two). I also joined with colleagues in turning out features, 'profiles', diary paragraphs: everything just like a real newspaper. (Sometimes we managed to sell pieces to the national press.) We had eager photographers and sports writers, and would-be political correspondents who wrote about the would-be politicians of the Union. We designed elaborate layouts, and each week we saw our paper through the press, learning and nonchalantly using as many of the technical terms of printing as we could absorb. I have never enjoyed newspaper work as much before or since.

When I was due to leave the university I wrote to all the Fleet Street editors and also to the editor of what was then the *Manchester Guardian.* The Fleet Street editors replied very briefly to my letters, saying they had no jobs to offer. The editor of the *Guardian* was then the late A. P. Wadsworth: a brilliant, infuriating and most lovable man. He didn't reply. I wrote to him again a fortnight later, reminding him of my letter. He still didn't reply.

Then came the day when I, a married student was threatened with court proceedings by the local Gas Board for non-payment of a bill which, in fact, had, with much effort, been paid. I sat at the typewriter, rolled up my slevves, and wrote a scorching letter to the Gas Board. By the time I'd finished it, I was thoroughly warmed up, and in the mood to compose more scorchers. I remembered the editor of the *Manchester Guardian* and wrote him an angry letter which concluded, as nearly as I can remember: 'Kindly regard my application as cancelled. I should prefer to work for an editor who has the courtesy to answer his correspondence.' I don't recommend this as the way to get a job on a newspaper. But it was probably the only way I could have got one on the *Manchester Guardian* at that time.

Back by return of post came a letter from Wadsworth inviting me to Manchester for an interview, after which I was offered a place on the staff.

Before it was time to start on the *Guardian*, I filled in for a few weeks by working on a London evening paper. That was an alarming experience. The whole editorial staff, from the editor downwards, worked in one enormous room under artificial lighting with typewriters clacking, telephones ringing, and shouts of 'Boy!' (to call a messenger) rising above the din. The pressure was incredible. At that time the paper produced nine editions a day (I think it's more now). There was the Mid-day Edition, which went to press at 9.05 a.m. followed by the Late Edition at 9.45, followed in turn by an edition called Final Night at 10.30 a.m. which went out to places a long way from London. The Final Night was followed by the Lunch Edition, for sale on the London streets. And so it went on through a succession of late extras and night finals until the last edition of all, at about 4.15, after which the reporters were busy working on stories for the next day's paper.

I did most of my reporting on the telephone; there wasn't often time to go out of the office on a story. I remember talking on the phone to a police station near to which a London motor-coach had crashed, and passing on the information the police gave me, a sentence at a time, to a man who took it down on a typewriter. It was wrenched from the machine—still a sentence at a time—and flashed round the sub-editor's table and on its way to the printers. The start of the story was probably being set up in type before I'd got to the end. The hurry wasn't always as great as that—though it wasn't really exceptional—but certain reporters didn't have time for fancy writing. For my first fortnight on that paper I had a perpetual headache. After that I got more or less used to it. But I don't think I was ever very brilliant as an evening-paper reporter; the pace was too fierce. I shall never know whether they'd have sacked me if I hadn't been due to leave of my own accord.

After that, life on the *Manchester Guardian* seemed peaceful. I had wanted to be a reporter or editorial-writer, but whenever I told A. P. Wadsworth this he would reply that reporters and editorial-writers were ten-a-penny and that the best prospects in journalism lay with the back-room boys who put the paper together and brought it out. I dare say he was right, but it was frustrating advice to give to any young man. Anyway, I spent four years as a sub-editor; one of the people who check and, if necessary reshape the reporters' work, write headlines for it, and prepare it for the printer with instructions about type sizes and column-widths.

On popular papers it's sometimes said that the sub-editor is king and the reporter merely feeds him with raw material. I don't think that's true. It certainly wasn't so on the *Manchester Guardian*, which was always a writer's paper. We were not silly enough to lay impious hands on the copy that came in from Alistair Cooke, Neville Cardus, Philip Hope-Wallace, Norman Shrapnel and other leading lights. Our creative role was limited to devising headlines; and *Guardian* headlines in those days were apt to be a bit staid and deadpan. Once we had a striking story about a French Senator, representing one of France's tropical colonies, who set off on a journey up a jungle river and was never heard of again. FRENCH SENATOR DISAPPEARS, said the *Guardian* headline, and underneath, in smaller type, 'Eaten by his Constituents?' I wonder whether he was. I shall never know.

Actually headline-writing can be an art, though admittedly a minor one. There was a lovely three-decker in the *Daily Express* at the time of the Suez trouble some years ago. The story was about a group of girls who'd travelled out to marry British soldiers, were allowed briefly on shore for the wedding ceremony, and were then shipped straight back to Britain for their own safety. The headline went:

Ship-to-shore girls wed.
Red roses and Sten guns for seven Suez brides
And home again today.

I've always felt that was a perfect short poem. You could analyse its rhythm and symbolism, just like any poem that might turn up in an O-level English syllabus. We never quite matched it, although occasionally a little quiet wit could get into a *Guardian* headline. There was one story about a huge crate, supposed to contain goods from Britain, which was opened in New York and found to be empty. INVISIBLE EXPORT, said the headline.

The bane of the headline-writer is always that he must put what he has to say into a given number of letters: A single-column headline, especially in a popular paper which uses large type, can be very restricted in the number of letters to a line. I remember one that was written in six lines, with a maximum of three letters to a line:

RAF
TO
GET
NEW
ACE
JET

That's a poem of a sort, too, I suppose. At least, it rhymes. And I was told (but I haven't seen it with my own eyes) that a headline had been written in lines of only two letters each:

KO
BY
OX.

After four years of sub-editing I became the *Guardian's* picture editor. I had to arrange for pictures, mostly of news and sport to be taken by our own photographers, and also had to choose from among the photographs sent in by freelances and picture agencies. And having got the pictures I wanted, I had to bargain for space in the paper to display them. This could be very frustrating, expecially with sports pictures. If there was a day of dreadful weather, and most fixtures were called off, the sports editor would have wide open spaces to fill, and would be crying out for pictures; but, for the same reason, there wouldn't *be* any. If there was a good day's sport there would be plenty of pictures, but the sports editor would have so much excellent copy that he'd hardly be able to spare any space.

In the nature of things, news tends to happen suddenly, and it's a miracle if a photographer is there on the spot. That's why you don't see in your paper a picture of a smash-and-grab raid actually happening; all you see is a picture of the hole in the shop window. You don't see a picture of an express train crashing through a level-crossing barrier; you see a picture of the wreckage afterwards. A great many news photographs are pictures of what I call non-events: visiting statesmen being greeted at London Airport, or people receiving awards for this-or-that, or pretty girls employed at some exhibition in the hope of making it look less dull. Now that we're in the television age it often seems to me that newspaper photography is obsolete, and that pictures are mostly used for convenience in designing the page. If I were an editor today I'd be tempted to throw them all out and use nothing but maps and graphs, which at least can help the reader to understand what's going on.

From being picture editor I graduated to the editorship of the *Guardian*'s weekly international edition. This was, and is, mainly, but not entirely, a selection of the best material from a week's issues of the daily paper. It circulates mostly abroad, and in North America sells far more copies than any other British publication. I liked this job of selection, and it allowed me to make up my own paper just as I wished, with the satisfying feeling when the week's work was over that there was something to show for it: a brand new crisp clean issue. But a job like this is out of the mainstream of a paper. Just occasionally it was possible to write something for the daily paper. I used to claim (too hopefully, perhaps) that I could do any job on a newspaper except that of music critic or sports reporter, and that if really pushed I'd have had a good shot at those.

And yet . . . as time went by I felt I wanted to do something more permanent, something that wouldn't just be thrown away or used to wrap fish and chips, something that might still be read next month or even in ten years' time. So I started writing books. That's another story, and I can't tell it here. The books took up more and more space in my mind, more and more time out of my leisure, until at last I had to choose between authorship and journalism. I chose authorship.

But once you've been a journalist, there's a sense in which you're always a journalist. I find myself still 'looking for the story' in the events that go on around me. I still feel a tiny surge of excitement whenever I hear the fire-engine bell, and have to resist an impulse to break into a run to see what's happening. I think of the *Guardian* as 'we', not 'they', and shall probably do so until my dying day. (Actually I still keep a small part-time connection with the paper as children's books editor.) When I make my yearly income tax return, I describe myself as 'author and journalist'. If, as sometimes happens, I send information about something to the local paper of the town where I live, I write it up for them in the form of a news story and watch as anxiously as any reporter to see whether it gets into the paper unchanged.

'Well,' said the last youngster to whom I talked about my career in journalism, 'if you had your time back, would you do it again?'

'Not on your life,' I said promptly. 'I'd go into teaching, or accountancy, or a bank. Much better prospects.'

He looked disappointed. Of course, he didn't know about my policy of discouraging anyone who can possibly be discouraged.

'I think I shall try it all the same,' he said.

Good luck to him if he does. He'll need it. He'll also need energy, persistence, and great physical toughness, as well as talent and all the education he can get. Journalism's an occupation that demands just about everything you have. Some people can give their all to the job, gladly. If you're one of those take the advice of an American President. He was talking about politics, but it applies to journalism too. 'If you can't stand the heat,' he said, 'keep out of the kitchen.'

MACFADYEN'S SHIRTS
by Iona McGregor

Phemie had worked for six weeks at the debtor's lodging-house when Mr. MacFadyen arrived. She hardly noticed him at first; she had been miserable ever since Mrs. Bain had taken her from the Edinburgh Orphans' Hospital.

For years she had been sure that her parents would come to claim her on her fourteenth birthday, the day she had to leave the Hospital. She dreamed of a fine house where she would wear silk and muslin, and lie in bed until noon.

Instead, she now rose at six, washed fifty stone steps every day, and cleaned the debtors' rooms. Worst of all was the Monday evening supper.

Every Monday Mrs. Bain bought a creel of plump oysters and two gallons of porter, and added it to her fourpenny supper. The debtors became very merry as the evening wore on. On her first Monday, Phemie served them and then sat in dumb misery with a stuttering schoolmaster, a broken wine-merchant, and a high-coloured actress who claimed to be cousin to the Duchess of Gordon, and a half-dozen more. After half an hour Phemie burst into tears and left the room. She would not eat the haddock that Mrs. Bain put aside for her later.

When Mr. MacFadyen arrived, Phemie was not pleased to

see him. He meant only another room to clean. But Mrs. Bain glowed with pleasure. Even in the Sanctuary, it was hard to let her top attic, where the rafters leaked and the rotten window-frame was stuffed with rags.

Mr. MacFadyen was delighted with the room. 'Admirable, madam. Exactly the view I need!' he exclaimed in a Highland lilt. He was a plump young man with bright, popping eyes and a jauntily unkempt wig. He skipped to the window to peer at the slate roofs, now blurred with October mist, and the back-yards of the other lodging-houses that huddled like beggars at the entrance to Holyrood Palace. The view had no charm except for its promise of safety in the precincts of Palace and Abbey.

Mrs. Bain punched the straw mattress into a look of comfort. 'One shilling a day, sir, with two meals found, and a penny more if I wash your shirts.'

Mr. MacFadyen smirked. 'No washing, I thank you. I have—er—other arrangements.'

For the first time Phemie's face lighted with interest. Mr. MacFadyen had not the sly, cowed look of the other debtors; he seemed like a man on holiday.

'I hope, sir,' said Mrs. Bain, 'you dinna take your shirts up the hill to be washed on the Sabbath. This is a Godfearing house.'

Mr. MacFadyen chuckled, and hugged the long, brown cylinder under his arm. He fidgeted from one small foot to the other, plainly hinting at their departure. Mrs. Bain curtseyed and went; Phemie lingered and saw him whisk a long brass object from the cylinder, and point it through the window. He turned and caught her staring. Phemie blushed, but he blew her a kiss, and gave a charming wink as she fled.

For several days Phemie put enormous effort into cleaning Mr. MacFadyen's room. She stretched the sheets as taut as a drumskin; she even swept away the pigeon-droppings on his window-sill. Her fingers ached to open the mysterious cylinder.

On Thursday morning Mr. MacFadyen skipped into the room as she was polishing his leather valise. 'Phemie, Phemie, *mo chridh*,' he exclaimed, 'you are rubbing away your bonny wee hands for me! If only I could show my gratitude—alas, I have not a bawbee to my name. I cannot think how I'll pay good Mistress Bain at the end of the week.'

Phemie warmed with pity. 'Och, sir, I like fine to sort your room, and I have my wages.'

'Wages?' His voice sharpened, then mellowed to its usual tone, rich and dark as heather honey. 'A penny a day, no doubt,' he muttered.

Phemie's heart fluttered at her own boldness. 'Sir, please to tell me. What's *yon*?' She pointed to the cylinder.

Mr. MacFadyen laughed and pulled the long piece of brass from its case. 'A telescope, Phemie.'

'Whatna kind of beast would that be?'

He led her to the window and fitted the instrument to her eye. 'Have a keek, my dear.'

Phemie gasped as she saw chimneys a handsbreath away, and a pigeon's eye staring balefully into her own. Beyond the burying-ground, she could identify every garment spread out to dry on the Calton Hill. She screamed with excitement.

'Sir, the washing! All they fine shirts, Mr. MacFadyen!'

Mr. MacFadyen groaned, and Phemie dropped the telescope in consternation. 'What ails you, sir?'

'Shirts,' he said bitterly, 'there's always fine shirts up there on a Thursday. Look!' He undid his tattered velvet coat and threw it open. Phemie modestly turned away, but not before she had seen the golden hair curling on Mr. MacFadyen's chest. He buttoned his coat and frilled his neck-cloth to hide the gap. 'Is it not black shame that a gentleman born should be so naked? And my own father stood by the Prince at Culloden!'

'Oh, sir,' breathed Phemie, 'I'm sore at the heart for you.'

Mr. MacFadyen patted her hand. 'It's plain you have gentle blood in you, Phemie.'

Phemie flushed with pleasure, and said timidly, 'I'd give you a shirt if I could, sir, even if I had to take it from my mistress. It's no right for them up there to have so many, and you without a single one.'

Mr. MacFadyen sighed. 'I'll be arrested if I go outside the Sanctuary except on the Sabbath. And there's no washing then.'

He shivered and dragged the coat round his ribs. 'If only I had some brave and generous friend, *mo chridh*—I saw some bonny ones through my telescope just now, lying behind a whin-bush.'

Phemie's voice trembled as she said, 'I'll go up and lift a shirt for you, Mr. MacFadyen.'

'Two, Phemie,' said Mr. MacFadyen softly. 'I am a gentleman, remember. I change my shirt every day.'

It was easier than Phemie had expected. The servants sent to guard the clothes were more interested in their own gossip; they could relax, because there was no wind to blow away the washing that starred the hill-side like snowy manna. So Phemie edged round the hill without being noticed. She stooped to clutch a linen sleeve, and stowed the first booty in her covered basket. Success made her bold, but not careless. Soon she had six fine shirts tucked out of sight.

She had spent nearly an hour on the hill, and Mrs. Bain would be suspicious if she stayed longer. Phemie was panting from exhilaration and an almost pleasurable tang of fear; but she looked round for yet another shirt, one finer than the rest, that Mr. MacFadyen could wear on Sundays.

Suddenly she saw it, elegantly spread over a boulder. It was lace-frilled at sleeve-ends and bosom, with a gold thread worked into the seams. She grasped it eagerly and crammed it into the overfull basket. She did not notice that one sleeve trailed over the edge.

She had passed the crest of the hill and was hurrying by the graveyard, when she heard a raucous shout.

'Come back, you thieving limmer! Stop her! Thief, thief!'

Phemie looked back in panic and saw three servant-girls against the skyline. She picked up her skirts and ran. The girls clattered down the path behind her, and chased her along the back of the Canongate, screaming abuse. Phemie darted into one of the dark alleys and hid half-way up a turnpike stair until they had gone. Then she crept back to the lodging-house, as happy as any debtor to see the Sanctuary cross.

Mr. MacFadyen capered round his room with joy when she gave him the shirts. At the sight of the gold thread-work on the

seventh, he whirled Phemie off her feet, crying, 'Three guineas at least, *mo chridh*!'

Phemie blushed and asked, 'Three guineas? What do you mean, sir?'

Abruptly, he put her down and snapped, 'Never heed. It was blethers I was speaking then.' Then he saw her downcast look, and patted her shoulder. 'You're a great wee lassie, Phemie. . . . Off you go, now.'

Phemie was so happy that she forgot to mention she had been chased off the Calton Hill. Later in the day, when she remembered, she smiled to herself: she would tell him another time. He had guessed she had gentle blood; they would have many secrets to share.

At supper that evening, Mr. MacFadyen unbuttoned his coat to display the white linen beneath. He winked at Phemie across the room, but was too busy to speak to her. On Friday and Saturday he was strangely elusive. Phemie still smiled; she was waiting in happy impatience for Sunday, to see him in the full glory of his gold-threaded shirt.

On Sunday morning, Mr. MacFadyen appeared in plain linen. Phemie stopped him on the staircase and said, 'Sir, I wanted you to wear the fine one on the Sabbath. That's why I lifted it for you.'

He looked down haughtily from the higher step. 'Hold your wheesht, you foolish child, and do not be blabbing so loud.'

Tears sprang to her eyes at his unkindness. 'That's a fine way to speak,' she reproached him, 'after all the trauchle I was at for your shirts. They near on caught me, running down the hill.'

Mr. MacFadyen's plump face purpled. 'What? You stupid, stupid lassie! Why did you not tell me before?' He left her hastily, and slammed his door behind him.

The next morning, the lodgers appeared one by one as usual to take their breakfast, and then loiter away the day in the Sanctuary. But not Mr. MacFadyen. When the town clocks struck eight, Mrs. Bain went upstairs and knocked on his door. After a few minutes she ran down to the kitchen.

'MacFadyen's flitted!' she cried indignantly, 'and he owes me six days' rent!'

'Oh!' wailed Phemie. She was stricken with misery, because he had gone without saying goodbye. 'Are you sure he's no there, mistress?' Tears began to trickle down her cheeks.

Mrs. Bain told her sharply not to greet over bad rubbish, and sent her to buy the day's vegetables from the kail-wives at the Tron. Phemie lingered over her errand, hoping to see Mr. MacFadyen lurking in some alley. She did not find him in the Canongate or High Street, and on her way home went to search the Cowgate. She peered tearfully into the old clothes shops there, twitching aside the racks of coats and breeches, as if Mr. MacFadyen had somehow concealed himself in a hanging suit of livery.

Outside the very last shop she saw a young officer jabbing

with his sword at a gold-threaded shirt that dangled above the door.

'Bring it down, bring it down at once! . . . Ah!' Triumphantly, he caught the neck-band on his point and flicked down the shirt. The shop-keeper came to the door. 'This is mine, madam,' said the officer. 'How dare you expose it for sale?'

'You'll pay to take it away,' retorted the woman.

'Never! You are a receiver of stolen goods, and I shall send the magistrates to you.' He marched away with the Sunday shirt that Phemie had taken for Mr. MacFadyen.

'I might have kent it,' said the shop-keeper gloomily.

Phemie stammered, 'How did you get the shirt, mistress?'

'A sleekit Highland rogue sold it to me—and a fine tale he told! Well, I'll just send the magistrates after *him*. They'll easy find out where he's been lodging.'

Phemie went pale. She dropped the vegetables in the road and took to her heels. As she ran, her eyes gushed with tears for what Mr. MacFadyen had done with her present; but behind her pain was the rising beat of fear. What if the magistrates came to the lodging-house and discovered the other shirts? And then found out that she had stolen them? 'Thief, thief!' the servant-girls had shouted. She would be whipped and put in prison.

In a frenzy of terror, Phemie stumbled up a flight of steps into the Canongate, ran down the crowded street for half a mile, and flung herself sobbing through the door of the lodging-house. She collided with Mrs. Bain and clung to her, gulping for breath, finding an unexpected comfort in the landlady's ample body.

"Mistress, up the stair—is there any—can I keek in his room?'

Mrs. Bain seemed to understand her nonsense. They went upstairs together; Mrs. Bain stood in silence while Phemie ran round the room looking in vain for the shirts.

"Where have they gone?' she cried in anguish. 'I've got to find them mistress, I've got to find them!'

'What's all this steer, Phemie?' asked Mrs. Bain mildly. 'Are you missing something?'

Phemie twisted her hands in her skirts, and came over to her slowly. 'I'll have to tell you,' she whispered.

'Aye, you'd best,' said Mrs. Bain, but in a kind voice. Phemie began her story, hesitated, broke out weeping several times, and in the end, told it.

'Dinna send me to the jail, mistress!' she pleaded.

Mrs. Bain folded her hands. 'Mistress Minto's Betty was here while you were out, and a wheen other lassies, too. They were looking for their masters' shirts.

Phemie whimpered in despair.

'I told them I had a daft young servant-lass who didna ken my washing from other folk's, and had lifted six shirts by mistake, I gave them back to the lassies, Phemie.'

Phemie cried out in relief, and then threw herself once more at Mrs. Bain's apron. 'Thank you, thank you, mistress. What a muckle fool I've been!'

'Aye, he's a rascal, yon MacFadyen. The lassies said he's been at the same ploy all over the city, but they canna catch him."

Phemie tossed her head. 'Och, I'll not fash myself about him again . . . I'm that happy—'

Mrs. Bain briskly cut her short. 'Get your mop and dusters, Phemie. We canna stand blethering all the day.'

Phemie hurried downstairs laughing; she looked round the friendly kitchen, and gave a sigh of joy.

'It's oysters and porter tonight,' she thought. 'I aye had a mind to try them. Yon nice wee dominie, he wanted me to take a sup with him last week. I wonder would he give me some tonight?'

She began to sing as she took her bucket out to the well.

THE PERGOLA
by William Mayne

How difficult to make the mood fit the inspiration. Alan Farndale often found it so, on the edge of bedtime, when he began to be inspired. He thought of dawn coming like milk into the sky, and wrote 'Night has closed his cloudy eye,' and saw that he was astray in the first line. 'Day has opened his cloudy eye' was no good, because the word cloudy set the whole tone of the line, but at the same time gave the effect of weariness to whatever had that eye. So day could not open his eye already cloudy; and for night to close his eye at all was to make darkness darker yet. The mood, which was dawn, had to go, and the inspiration, which was the line, had to stay, and be transferred to dusk: 'Day has closed his cloudy eye.' Alan let the line wander for a moment, remembering the things he should be doing instead of writing a poem; and then let them go again: algebraic factors, things that inspired Mr. Markham with the fervour Alan felt when he wrote a verse. Mr. Markham would work his example forwards and backwards, change its numbers and signs, achieve a result that seemed, to Alan, to have no connection with the working, and set a number of the things for prep or immediate work, convinced that the form shared his rapture. Now, at this moment, there were six of them in an exercise book, waiting to be translated into their final forms. Alan had let them sleep, and brought out instead the book where the verse went, and used his pencil lead on that instead.

'Day has closed his cloudy eye.' Why not make it an iambic line, starting 'That day'? Only four feet, te dum, te dum, te dum, te dum. There would be a fitting rhyme in the third line, matching the implicit slumber: 'lie'. But would a four foot line do? He tried a row of them in his mind, and they went on and on, jogging, peeling off like pencil sharpenings. He tried four and three, four and three, but that came out trite and tripping, like the schooner Hesperus with the bowsprit missing. He tried a five foot line, and that was what the blood wanted, because it instantly made the first line carry over. 'The day has closed his cloudy eye. There is between the te dum and the dark te dum' 'There is between the curfew' whatever a curfew is 'and the night a time' which gave another carrying over, which was too much. Besides, the curfew had instantly made the whole poem into Gray's Elegy, which is the chief danger in five-foot iambic lines about the dusk.

The night itself, coming at the window, was no help, because there was too much of it. The window looked north, into the place where the sun had set. It had gone down behind the houses, leaving a stain in the sky. The houses stood at the edge of sight, looking, with their regular roofs and equal chimneys as if they had been hung on an invisible line. Below, in the garden, there was light hanging round the roses still, and an even shadow without boundaries on lawn and wall and flower bed. At the end of the garden lay the alley, between its brick walls, and that was the only dark trench in the landscape. The air was still: the wind was breathing neither in nor out. On either side the gardens lay entranced. This is the poem, Alan thought, but words are no use for it. This is the faery land forlorn, but so many places were, because that land was undifferentiated, ungeographical: it was a land in the mind, and this was a land in the eye.

In the garden next door something moved, pale in the grey light. It was the top of Mr. Merton's head, bald and reflecting.

He had been sitting in the garden. Alan watched him fold his deck chair and go indoors. In the garden beyond that some white thing moved, a big dog, perhaps, going up and down the lawn, or path. Alan thought it might be washing, but there was not the wind to move hung clothes. In the houses opposite, whose backs looked across the gardens to the backs of the Mundy Street houses where Alan now was, there were squares of light of different colours, where the curtains shone.

Gray's Elegy would have been different, Alan thought, and then decided that Gray was the difference, because he was a different person. Alan was not looking at the nightfall for soliloquy's sake, or for the atmosphere of the moping owl, or for the sake that it was falling asleep; but rather because it was just waking. Now the gardens were the secret places, and in them might be anything now, or anyone: did there walk there that inspiration personified that he felt swell in him so often of a sudden; that unknown, unlooked-for jerk of the springs within turning the scenes he had visited familiarly into new lands?

But what happened each time was that the centre of it all evaded him. Each time he thought he had laid hands on it; and each time the muscle slackened and the hour of the marvel was over. There was no re-awakening at the thing itself, only the remembering of it. So it was now, and for the moment the gardens were immortal, and the gods wandered there. Then they too vanished. Alan held the moment, and it melted like a flake of snow. Whilst he had it there was no need of a poem, and then, when it had gone there was no way of writing one. If the words would have come he would have written, but the words went with the gods. He stayed by the window, looking out.

Mr. Merton had gone in. There was light from his downstairs window, and his shadow on the patch of brick paving outside the window. Alan wondered what he did, apart from looking over the wall on Saturdays and saying harmless silly things about nothing in particular. Beyond was the white movement in the further garden, the next but one, the house that had been empty. Perhaps they had a large energetic dog.

'As full of energy as the sun, but not so bright', would make a line, though energy was the wrong word. Virtue might be better, if it meant anything. Alan found that the meaning in poems was apt to be retrospective and had to be devised after the poem was written. Was Thomas Gray astonished at himself when he re-read those many pages?

The dog, if it was a dog, as full of . . . what? running, perhaps, as the sun, but not so bright, went into the house in whose garden it had been. That suits the moon, Alan thought. If the moon was the sun's dog, it would be as full of running and not so bright; but would it be captive in a garden? Yes, if the stars were the garden. The trouble was that the idea hadn't come as a poem, except for the one line.

Mother was upstairs then, to put his light out, and the poem went, and non-words, with non-meanings, came back to his mind: Mr. Markham's algebra.

The morning had the dewy breath of June: night had shaken a damp brush over the houses. The air was still again, and in the gardens sun and shade were still the simile for day and night. Alan fussed round mother, she was ironing a white shirt for him. Between his fussing he was writing down answers that looked hopeful for the algebra. He had the feeling often that arithmetical problems were worked out by the sleeping brain, and the answers could be written down at breakfast. He had not yet proved that the brain knew its work; or, if it did, then Mr. Markham's worked a different way. Likely figures and letters dripped on to the page, and he filled in the signs by intuition.

The ironed shirt he rolled up at once, and mother sighed, but it had to go into the saddlebag. The algebra went into the satchel, and he was ready to go. He rode on the pedal down the garden as he was being a ship. The door into the alley was a lock gate into the canal. He let himself through, called to them to cast off forrard, and went slowly down the alley, shaking the satchel down his back to its best place. The alley swung to the north and back again, where it went round the well that used to supply water, and then went straight, across the plain, perhaps, to the estuary.

At the estuary there was a buoy or bollard, which he moored

himself to with one hand whilst he waited for the traffic to leave. Whilst he waited he ran the sails down and started the engine, because sailing was not safe in the road. Then he cast off again, went through the breakers, which were the cobbles at the entrance to the alley and the step down into the road, and got into the current, and duelled with an ocean-going bus half way to school, and then went off upstream into a creek, at the end of which were the docks of school.

Mr. Markham was querulous about the workings of Alan's sub-conscious mind. 'It's the way to do football pools, perhaps, Farndale, but not the way to do algebra. No dividend. In fact, do them again.'

The sympathy of the staff was not with him, but Oscar Tullibund, who sat next to him, provided answers and workings, so that at the end of break Alan knew how to do them for himself, if nothing else better was in his mind.

Mr. Markham was better on the cricket field, and gave Alan Not Out, l.b.w. to a ball Alan himself would have agreed to if there had been no umpire. He stayed in and made eight before giving slip a gentle catch whose bowling, hitting and holding would not have harmed an egg.

'The thing is,' said Tullibund, when Alan was back at the pavilion, and they were lying on the grass in the smell of the cricket bags balancing bats on one finger; 'the thing is she won't look at me.'

Girls were Tullibund's perpetual problem. He marked down his prey, observed its habits, and then laid wait, but so far there was no catch to report. Alan listened to him slightly bored: Tullibund's forays were only of academic interest to him. Girls were girls and a weaker being. He could not see why Tullibund should want to dilute his experience with such flavourless stuff.

'You needn't drop that on my head,' said Alan, thinking though of Bagheera's moan when he lost Mowgli, 'put dead bats on my head, give me black bones to eat.' Tullibund took the dead bat and raised it again.

'It's true,' he said. 'She looks the other way.' He himself looked at Alan sideways in case there was any need to drop the bat again. 'Still, it doesn't matter,' he said. 'If you come to tea on Saturday, you know, just come, and we can get more things for Frogville.'

Frogville was Tullibund's engaging hobby, conducted in a corner of the garden, a damp spot, very suitable for its carrying out. Builders had left there a great heap of brick and tile, out of which Tullibund had made the little town of Frogville, and to which he had brought the reptiles that lived there. There were ponds and canals, with goldfish and newts and water-life, and in the brick and tile houses lived the frogs and toads, with groves of feverfew and groundsel, so that Alan always associated reptiles with the smell of weeds. Tullibund spend his week-ends in Frogville. Just now he was building a church, complete with bells. In fact he had started with the bells one wet day, and he thought he might train a rather intelligent toad to ring them. It was to be the cathedral of St. Salamander.

'I'll come,' said Alan. 'If you'll do all the touching, I don't like wrestling with frogs.'

'I've a golden newt, and a hedgehog,' said Tullibund. 'And a tortoise. And a bed of cress. I thought we could siphon the ponds.'

'I'll come,' said Alan. 'Wake up, they've drawn stumps.' Tullibund let the bat he was holding fall into its own shadow, and they went back to school.

In the evening, when Alan went to his room the sun had poured wine all over one wall. He left the light off and walked across the floor as if his blood was all in his skin, and from the casement watched the sun go down between the houses, inking them in clear and low and then being blotted out itself by the eclipsing chimneypots. Alan watched the colour go from his hands and then from the gardens. He looked to see what colour Mr. Merton's head was shining, but he was not there tonight. But in the garden beyond there was that same moving whiteness, and a second whiteness as well, which did not move, like a pillar standing in the garden among the bushes. Then someone called in that direction, and the moving white figure went in towards the house. Alan concluded it was a dog; but it had not barked yet, probably because the people had been there so short a time.

The next night there were three of the tall white things, and the night after, having dreamt about them, he went up earlier to look, and saw in the daylight only what he had seen in the dusk: tall white posts, too close together to be posts for washing lines. They were no more than that. The large white dog was not there in the garden to be seen. Alan did not look particularly in that direction again, because the mood of looking out of the window went after he had taken out a fresh set of library books.

But on Saturday evening he did look out, whilst he went through in his mind what the day had held: siphoning the ponds of Frogville and training the toad to ring the bells. Next week Tullibund intended to go out into the country and catch snakes. He was to read a book about it beforehand. Then the snakes coiled away from Alan's mind, when he looked along the gardens, and saw what was in the one belonging to the next house but one.

Instead of two or three posts white among the plants, there was a double row of them, and bars across making an archway in each pair. The double row led from the house to a round structure, white again, with a pinnacle; and in the pinnacle was a light. There was some other white thing running up and down the avenue. It was not a dog, but a girl. She had a dog with her, but it was a small brown one, not a large white one: she was what he had thought a dog. His poem was spoilt. No more was 'that dog as full of running as the sun, but not so bright' part of a poem. The dog died, and with it went all the flock of rhymes gathered for it. It was no good having the private moon tangled with other people's kids who had been deceiving him by running up and down in the dark, even if they had a dog for satellite.

It was getting darker minute by minute, and he could see less and less of the structure and more and more of the light. After a time he put his own light on and went to bed.

The next day was Sunday, and he was late up, and never had the opportunity all day to look out of his window in daylight, so that by dusk he saw it again, and there was no one in the garden, and no light in the pinnacle. On Monday morning he could have looked, but Monday is a day slow to start, and it took him all his going to get out of the house in time at all. It wasn't until he went past that garden in the alley that he thought of the sprung-up pinnacle, and the wall was too high for it to be seen, and there was no time to try looking from further away. He was not himself and awake until he was in the wake of a delivery van lumbering down the road like a stern-wheeler.

Tullibund was in a dream of pleasure all day because his girl had spoken to him that morning. She had only said 'Get out, you gapy kid,' but to Tullibund they were words as fair and momentous as any that came from Sinai, though he had, of course, no intention of obeying them. But he said that nothing would put him off the snakes on Saturday, except rain.

Alan came down through the afternoon traffic, and Tullibund came idly with him as far as the end of the alley, going a longer way home because he had nothing better to do. Between them they were thinking of a joke about a science teacher, a woman, who, they thought, was asked what subject she liked best, and she answered that she liked geology and ecology, but snakes were her-pet-ology. Tullibund was the sort that saw jokes, but didn't find them funny. Even this one, though he had inspired it himself, and done a certain amount of work on it, had at first no humorous aspect. In fact it was not until he had left Alan that it tickled his humour, and then he drew in to a lamp post, held on to it, and giggled. Alan saw him skid to the side, and then heard him, and went to see what had happened to him. By then Tullibund was unable to repeat the joke without tears, a stage Alan was already through, so he could only stand there and smile.

It was a wake to Alan and a resurrection to Tullibund. Whilst they held this mixed ceremony a girl came by. Alan would not have noticed her, but Tullibund did. Before he could swallow his next sob and turn his head and look towards Mundy Street, the way she was going, she had gone. 'Only a kid,' he said. Then he thought of herpetology again, and was strangled by it.

Alan waited until he was sober, and saw him off, then went into the alley. The gate of the house with the pinnacle was open. He saw the white wood inside growing from the grass, and stopped his bicycle, leaned it against the wall, and walked back, looking in. But before he could see any more the girl with the brown dog stepped across and shut the gate, without seeing him. He had stopped to no purpose. He went on to his bicycle again and rode a little way, then turned back and put the bicycle where it had been, in the corner where the enclosure of the wall began to twist the alley. There were two sides to hold on to there, and he managed to climb up on to the cross-bar of the bicycle, and was just able to see across the top of the wall, without being able to see down the other side at all. He thought that the saddle might give him six inches, but all he gained was a scraped hand and a banged head when the bicycle went weak by the front wheel and lay down like a horse. He came on top of it, and sat there counting his limbs and watching the wheels spin. The door in the wall opened behind him, but he felt unable to look up and turn round. He stood the way he was facing and got on to the bicycle again, feeling as if he had been hammered and then watched with scorn, not even stopping to rub the grit off his hands until he was round the bend in the alley and out of sight of whoever it was watching.

He licked his wounded hand all the evening, waiting for mortification to set in, happily without knowing what it was. He imagined it was a sensation, or etymologically a lack of feeling. In the morning the thick of his hand was tender and there was still a bruise on his head, and there was a feeling, in neither head nor hand but at the heart, that climbing up to look over walls was a habit best forgotten as soon as made.

Whilst he ticked his way along the straight of the alley (with the electric engines of the Panama pulling) he heard another craft enter the canal behind him. There was nothing in that because all the houses either side had gates to the alley. The only consideration was that some old person might have come out who would object to cyclists in the narrow way. Alan knew of the objection, and went slowly always. He went on carefully, moored at the bollard, and waited for a gap to cross the road. Whilst he waited there, warming up the engines of a motor-torpedo boat, another cyclist stopped at the same place. It was the girl of the house with the pinnacle. She did not need to moor herself, but stepped down into her bicycle, waiting for a smaller gap in the traffic than Alan needed, because she was not going to cross the road. She looked at Alan, smiled like a neighbour, and went off between two vans. Alan was about to take off too when he heard a yap behind him, and then the scutter of feet. The brown dog was following the girl, and he was quite certain she did not know about him. She had gone now. Alan baled out and fielded the dog, or saved the goal, perhaps; and felt like Gerald Durrell capturing a badger or a large duck-billed platypus. The platypus licked his face in a truly friendly manner, and tried to climb on to his shoulder and get away. It was one of those dogs with a long straight coat and a pleasant woody smell. He brought it down off his shoulder and put it under his arm. It whimpered and ran with its legs, but they were in the air and took it nowhere. Alan gathered in his bicycle and put it further in the alley, where it would be safe, and walked back with the dog. There was a disc on its collar, naming the owner, West, with an address the other side of town, which would be right for the girl's house, since they had only just come.

The garden gate was open. Alan felt he could have looked in to see the white structure, but it would not be fair if he did. It seemed like cheating, like keeping a half-crown that someone thought they had dropped in the road and you had found in the form room. He put the dog through and closed the door.

Tullibund spent the day exchanging password and countersign with Alan. 'Natrix natrix natrix' was one, and 'Bufo bufo bufo' the other. Tomorrow, said Tullibund, it would be 'Troglodytes troglodytes troglodytes' and some other animal not yet found.

Alan was thinking most of the day of how he ought to have cheated and looked in at the West's garden gate. The chance had been given, and he had passed it by. There was no more looking over walls to be done; and now the only way seemed to be to open the gate boldly and look plainly; but that would be too plain, in fact. He thought he might have to ask the girl something, perhaps about the dog; but he was not sure what a girl might say. He remembered how he had first seen Tullibund with a pocketful of dead mice, mummified, and dug out of a chimney breast, found by Tullibund and a neighbour's cat, conscripted for the purpose, during alterations. He had been leaving the mice about the school, and had seemed to Alan heroic and original. It was the heroic aspect that fascinated Alan most, and held him away in awe. It had taken him half a term to speak to Tullibund, and then it was to offer him the use of a bicycle pump. Now they met at the school gate, and arranged Frogville on Saturdays. The heroism had departed, and Alan thought it was something different now. It was the same stuff that let Tullibund hold a toad and a sandwich in the same hand. It was not truly heroic quality, but indifference to some conventions. But the glamour had not all gone. It might be messy, even unhygienic, to mix toads with potted meat, but Alan himself could not even touch the toad, let alone hold it. Besides, Tullibund always seemed to have more activity in hand each day than Alan had in a year. It was Tullibund who made Frogville, who found out the chantable quality of Natrix natrix natrix, who had first been a ship in the seaways of the street, who had formulated the theory that the harder you worked in school the less work you had to do. Tullibund, in fact, did very well. He was always one ahead, ahead of Alan, at any rate. Alan thought he was probably more intelligent, but of course, had never thought of a poem in his life. Alan never said anything about verse to him, not knowing that Tullibund was proud of a poet's friendship, and was secretly expecting him to do poetic things and inspire them all to some high and unthought-of duty, and, later on, to wear a velvet cap, grow a beard, and be written in books.

Tullibund's advice would have been worth having, in the matter of the pinnacle, but Alan thought he would set his own seige. Tullibund, he felt, would go up to the front door, ask to look at the garden, examine it, and be sent on his way with a bunch of flowers, like the time when they had been poaching for newts and been caught by the owner of the pond and given honey for tea. Tullibund got results. Alan wanted the endeavour, not the achievement itself. He did not like to acknowledge his objective.

So in the afternoon he shed Tullibund at the gate of the

school and went home a different way, as fast as he could, and waited in the alley, making an imaginary adjustment to his brakes. His calculation was right. The girl came into the alley and rode past him. He had it in mind what to say. First something about the dog, then, leading off from that, a remark about the pinnacle. But he couldn't make the remark lead off from the dog: there was no connection. Besides, he should have begun by now, and not let her go past. Tullibund would have sprung into life by now, just by meeting someone else in a narrow way. He remembered, on the newt-catching expedition, how they had met a boy in a country lane, whilst they were still looking for the pond. Tullibund had said sharply, 'Where's the pond near the ruined chapel, you with the dirty face?' The little boy, on a tricycle too small for him, had looked squarely at Tullibund, then rammed him amidships with the tricycle, stared up at him with great intensity for ten seconds from close to, and said 'Follow me, pardner,' and led them along the road, telling them his life history, the number of his family, his address, his name, what he hoped to be in later life and the doctor's telephone number. Then he had left them at the stile and gone weaving back up the road. Later on that day they had been given honey for tea. Tullibund had an effect like that on people; except on his girl, who was silent towards him again. Alan did not want to be rebuffed.

He caught up with the girl at her gate, where she had stopped and got off. He stopped too, and she looked up and smiled.

'I put your dog in this morning,' he said.

'Are you Alan?' she said. 'Mummy said you wrote poems. I wrote one once and sent it to *Girl*, and they printed it in the paper.

Alan said nothing, because he was jealous at meeting a professional who was only a girl.

'It was about Nipper,' she continued. 'He ate a slipper, and then he ate a kipper, so the poem was easy, I just pretended he went to sea, like a tripper, on a boat with a skipper; and there were some more rhymes too. Shall I show it to you?'

'If you like,' said Alan. 'I mean, if you please.'

'You can come after tea,' said the girl. 'I'll be in the garden.' She gave him another smile, and went through the door.

Alan's professional jealousy vanished. He was grateful to her for mere politeness. Tullibund could not do better. In fact, Tullibund had done a great deal worse: all he had had was a remark about being a gapy kid, whereas Alan himself had been acknowledged as a poet, more than anyone would do (naturally) for Tullibund, and more than Tullibund had done for him.

After tea he walked down the alley again, and came to the gate. Now, after the poem had been read, he could enquire about the white pinnacle, and know the full meaning of it. He inclined to the view that the girl's father, Mr. West, had seen it in a dream, or observed it in a forest, sallying on some strange adventure spiced with witchcraft, and had built it to satisfy an urge to own something beautiful. To Alan there was nothing so beautiful in the gardens. The first question, though, was whether one had to knock at the garden gate that was quite solid. He concluded that one didn't, unless it was a castle gate. He turned the catch, and pushed the door open, and entered into the presence of the white building.

The pinnacle was in the middle of a six-sided roof of glass, supported on six columns set in the grass. Close to the thing was very plain and smaller than it looked from his window. To the house, from one side, stretched the double row of pillars with their joining beams across. From here the effect of an avenue was not so marked. Roses were tied round some of the pillars. Alan himself would have cleared away all growing things and let the pillars stand clear.

There was no one in the garden. Alan had a good look at the pinnacle from underneath. It was only the end points of the roof beams, rising to the centre of the glass roof, with a wooden band to hold them together, and a tiny spire and a ball to cap them. Out of the ball rose a wire, and that ran down to the earth for a lightning conductor. Inside there was a naked bulb. Alan was disappointed. He had been looking for carving and dragon's heads and arches, and all he had found was something like an unfinished bus shelter.

The girl came out into the garden from the house, and the dog came barking to him, until he was told to stop.

'I brought the poem,' said the girl. 'Do you like Daddy's pergola? Mummy and I hate it, but it might be useful for garden parties. We would rather have had a barbecue kitchen.'

'I wouldn't like roses growing on it,' said Alan.

'Mummy's going to get some more and cover it up,' said the girl. 'It'll look awful next year, don't you think?'

'It's like the sleeping beauty,' said Alan. 'With things growing on it.'

'Mummy says it's plebian,' said the girl. Whatever that meant, Alan thought, I'm not to argue with it.

The girl had the poem in the paper that had printed it. She gave it to Alan, and whilst he read it she went running round the six posts of the covered place with the dog. Alan found the verse a pathetic jingle. The only thing he could praise it for was its clear meaning, and he knew that was accidental, and came to suit the rhymes. He put the paper down by his side when he had finished, and the girl came running to see what he thought.

By this time he thought he knew her name, because it had been printed above the verse. To make sure he asked her.

'Of course it's mine,' she said. 'Only they don't call me Dorothy, but Dorrie. Did you like it?'

'Yes,' said Alan, because that was the right thing to say. 'You ought to write some more.'

'That's what Uncle Bill says,' said the girl. 'He says I'll have to write a lot more before I'm famous.'

Alan knew the remark about writing more was a safe one, because that was what Mr. Markham had told him to do. Though he was a teacher of mathematics he was the poetic one of the staff, much more so than Mr. Orton, who taught the subject English.

'Don't go yet,' said Dorrie. 'You can come and see our house. We're making it much nicer than it was. Mummy says it's very difficult to make anything of these houses, but she's going to do her best, with a lick of white paint here and there, and all the wallpaper books. She thinks she may have to go to London to get the right things. We have to do our best with the pergola. Daddy doesn't understand about style, you see.'

Alan soon learnt to follow-my-leader in his opinions of the rooms in the house. He was sure he might as well not say what he thought, because if he disagreed he would be thought unfit to be a poet, because poets obviously like the right things. The only room he liked was Mr. West's own, which he had decorated himself to his own liking. One wall was photographs from top to bottom, pinned on haphazard, because Mr. West was something to do with a newspaper. The other wall was green with two gas, fires in it. Another was all french window—'It looks out on to his precious pergola, doesn't it Daddy,' said Dorrie—and the fourth had a very solid bookcase pushed against it. The paint was brown, the carpet was brown, and the whole room smelt strongly of tobacco. Alan thought the pergola at its best from here, admired the brown paint because it looked comfortable, and thought the two gas fires the best heating arrangement he had ever seen. But he thought he ought to say nothing. Mr. West sat at a desk and smiled.

'He was born in Russia,' said Dorrie, looking at him as if he were an exhibit.

'Yes,' said Alan; to him the pergola was explained. It was a summer-house in a forest palace, and the bears were not far away, even if Mundy Street was nearer.

Alan went in a little while, because he had prep to do. Dorrie saw him out of the house, and he walked down the garden alone. When he looked back Mr. West was standing at his french window, and gave him a nod.

Alan looked out in the dusk as he went to bed. He saw Dorrie in the garden, running up and down with the dog inside the pergola. There were two places to see the pergola from, he thought: Mr. West's room, and from here. He knew it again as the thing he had first imagined, part of a palace. Mr. West had brought the idea palace back with him from Russia, and built it. The dog, which was Dorrie in the end, as full of running as the sun, but not so bright, could caper in the white palace of the Tsar, he thought again; but the dog, being Dorrie, was acting like Dorrie, as a princess, a princess that didn't know a palace when she saw one.

In the morning Dorrie was waiting for him at the garden door, and the warship Alan was in that morning had to doff its guns and be a cyclist. 'I thought you might be waiting,' she said. 'You could ride along with me.'

'You go a different way,' said Alan; but Dorrie thought that was no excuse, because he could go with her so far and cut across the streets. Alan, anxious to please whenever there was somebody there to be pleased, turned left with her at the end of the alley, and went her way—like a rowing boat, he thought.

Dorrie told him where he might turn off and proceed to school. You could meet me here,' she said. 'On the way back. I won't hurry, and then you can be here first.'

'Well, all right,' said Alan. 'Good bye for now.' He rode off a little astonished at himself, but deciding he would go back another way. However, he had not gone far when Tullibund laid an arm on his head and took his cap.

'Who's your sputnik?' said Tullibund. 'Back there.'

'Kid next door,' said Alan. 'She bossed me along this way today. Give us that cap, Tull.'

'Just wondered,' said Tullibund. 'Did you know what she was doing?'

'When?' said Alan. 'Tull, you great fool, you've posted it.' Tullibund had been playing with Alan's cap, to divert attention from what he had to say. In one of the longer reaches of his humour, coming out unawares now that he was thinking of something different, he had stuffed it into the opening of a pillar-box.

'It's gone,' said Tullibund. 'Just now. She was blowing great kisses at you.' He was sadly worried by the kisses, and to cover his worry he began to post his own cap, inch by inch, folded up like a Cornish pasty.

'Kisses!' said Alan. 'Don't be filthy, old boy. And that's your cap going too.'

'She was,' said Tullibund. 'Oh lum, it's gone too.' He put his eye to the opening. 'Didn't you know?'

'I only saw her last night,' said Alan. 'She's nobody.' But he knew it was a lie, because if she blew kisses to him then his heart was bound to notice. 'Just cheek,' he said. 'Why, anyway?'

'Just thought you might have been going off with her,' said Tullibund. 'Just thought you mightn't care about Frogville and so on. You were my friend first, not hers.'

'Oh, vive la Frogville et les crapauds,' said Alan. 'You needn't go red in the face about it.'

'Red in the face yourself,' said Tullibund.

'It's the pillar-box shining on us,' said Alan. But it wasn't the pillar box. They had each come out of their sockets, so to speak, and turned round once before settling in again. Tullibund was in firm again, but Alan had taken in a piece of grit and was not quite where he had been before. Kisses. 'We've had those caps,' Alan said. 'Better go on Tull. What about that hag of yours?'

Tullibund's girl was very different from Alan's girl. Tullibund's efforts were a part of Tullibund, and neither of them felt serious about them.

'I'm on the haughty today,' said Tullibund. 'Just raised my cap to her that's all.'

He had suppressed hysterics later on in prayers, and explained to Alan in the passage later that after raising the cap it was worn out and had to be thrown away, which was a joke; but it had suddenly struck him as comic that the caps were in the pillar-box at all. 'They'll come out pop pop,' he said, and collapsed in weakness. 'Postmarked,' he said, and had to be dragged into school.

In the afternoon he had to tell Tullibund that he was ordered to meet her again. Tullibund, recovered, understood perfectly calmly, and said he would think of a way of getting rid of her.

'I'll manage it,' said Alan, to comfort him; but thought at the same time that he would have to divide his attention and look both ways at once. If somebody likes you it is wrong to ignore them. Tullibund liked him, and he wouldn't be ignored, and the girl liked him. Alan couldn't see that the girl had any way of spreading into the part of him that was Tullibund's friend. She belonged to a new part that he had not noticed before. It was like having a good old vegetable Tullibund garden behind the house, and a girl flower-garden at the front. They didn't see each other.

'See you,' said Tullibund.

'Troglodytes troglodytes troglodytes,' said Alan.

Dorrie was at the corner first. 'I've been waiting for you so quickly that I'm out of breath.' she said.

'I've been coming along,' said Alan, and they rode back in silence to her gate.

'You can come when I've had my tea,' she said. 'I have such a lot of friends in and out usually, but now we've come to Mundy Street they haven't found me yet. Mummy and I don't really want them to come until the place is perfect. Mummy is so particular. But you live here, so you know what the houses are like.'

She stood in the doorway whilst he rode away. He thought of

looking back, but if he did she might be blowing him a kiss, and he had no idea what to do if she did. He had thought during the day of asking Tullibund, and then been certain that it was out of Tullibund's part of him.

After tea Dorrie had no idea what to do. First she played ball with him and the dog, and when the dog won she took him inside to look at pictures of horses, and then at all the family photographs. There were none of Russia, but there was no need of it; Alan felt the Russian part every time he saw Mr. West.

'This is a picture of me at our other house,' she said at last, closing the album. 'You can have it if you like.'

Two days ago Alan would have said plainly he didn't want it. Today he took it, said thank you, and put it in his diary. Dorrie sat looking at him. 'You should offer me one of you,' she said.

'I haven't got one,' he said. 'Except in the school group, and I was moving my head to talk to somebody else.' He had been about to mention Tullibund, until he found he was in a different compartment. To say he had spoken to Tullibund would hardly have been the truth, because the group, of two hundred and twelve, had been taken with a scanning camera, and Tullibund had skipped down from the back row when he had been done once to get to the other end and be done again, with the result that he had been taken not at all, because the camera was moving the other way.

When he went home, making his own way down the garden, he had no time to consider or look out of the window, because of the fresh library books. In the morning Tullibund was waiting out of sight for him, and caught him again by the pillar-box, without today daring to look at Dorrie, because it would upset him to see his friend being taken away. At school there was some discussion with the headmaster about two caps, delivered with the morning post. Nobody found it funny, except Tullibund, who saw the joke all over again, in spite of not being punished.

After school Alan had to say that he hadn't got rid of Dorrie yet, but that he would; and whilst he said it he knew it was a lie, told against his will, because something was binding itself to him with unasked-for affection, a grip he could not deny in his heart.

'O.K.' said Tullibund; and 'O.K.' he said the next night, and then turned to Alan again. 'Don't forget tomorrow afternoon,' he said. 'Snakes for Frogville.'

'She told me to go there,' said Alan, who had been waiting for this moment, unable to know what he would say. But the presence of Tullibund was the weight on the lever today. 'I'll tell her I've got to go out.' Tullibund nodded, and they went their different ways home.

'I'm going riding in the morning,' said Dorrie that evening; 'but you can come in the afternoon. I may have some friends, of course, but you won't mind, I suppose.'

'I can't come for long,' said Alan, thinking of the cool town of Frogville. 'I promised to go to a friend's house.' 'What for?' said Dorrie. 'Don't you see him at school?'

'It's prep, you see,' said Alan, which was true, because they read aloud to each other out of *A Tale of Two Cities*, in order to consume all three decks of the novel in the time they had.

Alan went to bed, with, if not a clear conscience, at least a plan ready for tomorrow. He looked out of the window once, and saw Dorrie in the garden still, and then looked out over the town, to that somewhere where Tullibund tended his citizens by torchlight, because they woke by night. Neither of them was so satisfying at the moment as the library book he had.

Early in the afternoon of the next day he rolled up his cycling cape, took his leather gloves out of the hall cupboard (for protection against snakes) and went off down the garden. There was rain in the air, softening in from the west, cooling the gardens. The breeze moved the flowers on their stems. He took his bicycle and went out into the alley.

He could get straight past Dorrie's gate, he felt. But he had promised to go in. Tullibund would be waiting now, rolling his newting net for the third or fourth time to a rule Alan had never been able to fathom, or lifting the roofs of Frogville to see how the colony was.

Alan opened the West's gate. There was no one in the garden, he thought, when he stepped in. Then, when he had closed the door behind him he found Dorrie was by the wall, and with her were two of her friends, two girls unknown.

'Oh, hello,' said Dorrie, but without any welcome. Alan felt himself smiling without wanting to and without doing it properly. He put his hand on the gate again.

'I was just going to see my friend,' he said.

'Don't let us keep you,' said Dorrie. 'If you've got to go, then by all means go.'

Alan could hardly understand her tone, because it was neither friendly nor sarcastic. It was polite, but nothing more.

'Goodbye, then,' said Alan, and went out of the door again.

The rain began to come, and he stopped just outside the gate to tug the cycling cape out of the carrier of the bicycle, so he heard without listening Dorrie's next words, in answer to a question he had not heard.

'Oh, he's a boy from the street here,' she said. 'He keeps coming round. Mummy and I can't understand it, but of course one has to be so patient with these people.'

Alan heard, put on the cape, and cycled through the rain to Tullibund's house.

'Ah,' said Tullibund. 'This is what they like. Before we go come and help me put the frogs out to soak. And there's a new river I've been making through St. Salamander Street. I want to see how it's working. I thought of a fountain, too, with water from the rain butt.'

Alan helped him with the frogs, putting on his gloves to handle them.

'They love to sit in the rain,' said Tullibund. 'They like to feel the rain on their backs.'

'I'm not always coming round, said Alan to himself in the falling damp, and thinking of a line 'And watercourse and runnel fill. With rush of fussing water chill'. But the line hovered useless. She invited me every time, he thought; and the frogs he was moving felt not only the warm rain but the warm salt tears that fell silent among them from his eyes.

I DON'T SEE GEORGE ANYMORE

by Philip Oakes

With the door of the greenhouse partly open we watched the sparrows perch on the fence at the end of the garden, and when they were settled and steady we shot them with the air-gun. The birds dropped on the other side of the fence and we collected them at the end of the morning. Sometimes we shot as many as twenty before dinner time.

The gun belonged to George, and the garden belonged to George's father. He paid us a penny for every sparrow we shot, because the birds ate his green peas, and he was a man who took pride in what he grew. The birds were fed (he put out crumbs and chains of nuts in the winter), and he felt they should be satisfied with what he provided.

He was not a cruel man. He was not even possessive. Probably, I think, he had an exaggerated sense of justice. 'What's right is right,' he would say, 'there's no getting round it,' and we were left with the feeling of an orderly world in which we were expected to behave with common sense and good manners, and bad luck on us if we broke the rules. He was a tall, red-faced man with hair like lint, quick tempered and affectionate. His wife, George's mother, was small and masterful, fond of her own pastries and never without a sweet in her pocket. She was fat but neat. Her hair was braided about her head, and her hands were square and scrubbed. She detested untidiness, and in the bus she had been known to pick a piece of cotton from the coat of the woman sitting in front of her. She hated loose ends.

Her house was small and warm, in winter as well as in summer. Metal sparkled, wood gleamed. There was always a smell of baking, and furniture polish. The coal fire never seemed to smoke, the hob shone like fresh tar. I spent more time there than at my own home. I felt its welcome contain me like a woollen jumper.

The garden was in a small-holding away from the house. It was surrounded by other allotments, planted with carrots and broccoli, and runner beans and tended by men who worked in the mills at the other end of town. In the evenings they came to the allotments and spent long hours over the plants, crumbling the soil between their fingers, sprinkling lime and derris powder and talking to each other over the low creosoted fences.

They never came to the allotments during the day, and it was then that the sparrows came to eat their fill, ignoring paper streamers, and strings of tin lids that were intended to scare them away.

We shot sparrows for the last week of the holiday before the summer term began, and between shots we sat on boxes in the greenhouse and smoked Woodbines, and debated what we would do when we left school at the end of the term. Inside the greenhouse it was close and prickly with the smell of dust and hot-water pipes wrapped in sacking. Small, green tomatoes clustered on the plants, as thin and hairy as old men's legs, and tiny red spiders scuttled over earth the colour of milk chocolate.

'I'll have to do something with my hands,' said George. 'I'll never manage in an office.'

'You could go in with your dad,' I said.

'I'd rather be on my own.'

George was a thin, bony youth with soft brown hair and a high polished forehead. He wore glasses which had cut a groove in the bridge of his nose. I was smaller, darker, given to violent enthusiasms and rebellions with which he sympathised, but never shared. We had been friends for three years.

The gun was older than either of us. The stock was carved from a block of walnut, and it was unlikely that it had been made for the gun. Sometimes we oiled and polished the wood until a clear, gold grain showed through and the gun felt wonderfully balanced and capable of tremendous slaughter. I think George loved the gun more than anything he had ever owned. He cared for it deeply and each time it passed between us it was a gift, an instrument not of killing, but affection.

We had been shooting sparrows for over an hour on a fine windy day when I saw the cat half way through the fence which separated the garden from the next allotment. It was a big black and white cat with a massive head and heavy shoulders and I watched it squeeze through the fence and stop suddenly when it saw the sparrows. It dropped its belly to the ground and slowly crawled along the fence bottom. It looked the biggest cat in the world, heavy and strong, and completely absorbed in its own business of reaching the birds. There seemed to be a cord between them which the cat was swallowing with a terrible, deliberate appetite. I imagined a reel in its stomach, turning without interruption. Inch by inch the distance lessened. The sparrows flirted their wings in the dust and squabbled. Their chirping was tuneless and blithe.

I put the gun to my shoulder and squeezed the trigger. The pellet struck the fence a little way in front of the cat, and drilled a hole in the creosoted wood so that an indented ring of yellow showed. The cat's plush face turned towards us, and the sun filled its eyes for a brilliant second. We saw its expression of utter outrage, and then it bounded into the rhubarb plantation.

Beneath the plateau of rhubarb leaves, flapping and ducking in the wind, it waited and watched us, and we stared at the red sticks of rhubarb, waiting for it to move. The high winds had swept the sky clean of cloud, and far above us swifts and martins flew in tight circles. Their screams reached us, tattered by the wind.

'Can you see it?' said George.

'Not yet.'

'I reckon it's gone.'

'Never.'

It was the waiting that did the damage, spicing the game with a new element. 'Bring it back alive,' said George, transformed in his mind's eye, into the prince of animal trappers.

'Too risky,' I said. 'It's a man-eater. Think of the villagers. Think what we promised. They'll never trust the white man again.'

We were both ardent picture-goers, Saturday-afternoon regulars at the Palace where Flash Gordon fought the Warlords of Mars, and Tarzan swung across jungle glades, a yo-yo in a loin cloth, his hunting knife at the ready. The animals were his friends, we knew that. But only the week before he'd been forced to do battle with a lion straddling its tawny back, wrenching its neck until the body sagged and the mailed paws turned to sponge.

'We'd better send the beaters in,' I said.

'Too dangerous,' said George. He picked up a pebble and threw it into the rhubarb. Something moved, and just as suddenly stopped. He tossed another pebble, and through the coral stems I saw a patch of black and white fur.

George saw it too. 'There it is, *bwana*.'

I hesitated. 'Do you think we should?'

'The natives are restless.' He pointed where he had thrown the pebble. 'May your bullet fly straight.'

I shot at the rhubarb and the pellet tore through several leaves flouncing the frilly edges and showing the white undersides. I fired three more pellets, hitting dirt, a garden fork, and then the cat. I knew the pellet had hit the cat by the sound of the impact. It was solid, positive thud which made me feel sick.

The game was over. George and I looked at each other and I gave him the gun. 'We've got to get that cat,' he said.

I knew what he meant. The cat was well-cared-for, and obviously came from a good home. If it went back injured there would be questions asked, and possibly we would be involved. At least we had to see how badly it was hurt.

The cat heard us coming and crawled away deeper into the rhubarb plantation. The wind dropped, and when the leaves stirred and we saw where it was hiding. We went to the other side of the plantation. Again, it heard our approach and crawled back the way it had come.

'We're getting nowhere,' said George. The swifts still screamed overhead, but with the drop in the wind there was a curious hush in the garden, and sounds from outside seemed to plop into it like pebbles in a pond.

We separated and walked into the plantation from opposite sides. I saw the cat about six feet to my left, and without thinking dived towards it. The leaves closed over my head, slapping my face as I went down. The cat darted away but I caught it by the tail, then by the scruff of the neck and held it close to the ground. The pellet had made a wound in its shoulder and its fur was wet with blood.

'We can't let it go like this,' I said.

George pushed his glasses back into the groove in his nose. He swallowed hard, and his adam's-apple climbed up and down. 'Is it really bad then?'

'See for yourself.'

He knelt beside me, and gently parted the cat's fur. As he'd said earlier, he was good with his hands. I remembered once finding a young blackbird with a broken leg. George had made a splint out of pipe spills and cotton, and for three weeks he had kept it in a shoe box, feeding it with chopped worms, giving it water from an eye-dropper until the leg was mended. He liked to mend things. It went beyond healing. He enjoyed restoring order. He was more like his father and mother than he imagined. He could not abide loose ends.

'I can't see the pellet,' he said.

'It's too far in.'

The cat growled deep in its throat, not in anger but as though it was reflecting on its bad luck and the impossibility of the situation. 'We could take it to the vet,' he said.

'They'd never let us shoot again.'

'Not if we told them what happened?'

'Never.'

I knew what he was thinking. I was having the same thoughts myself. I could almost hear George's father loud in disbelief, stern in judgement. Right was right and there was no getting round it. Unless, of course, we kept the whole rotten business to ourselves.

'Kill it,' I said, 'it's the only way.'

'You can't kill a cat with an air gun.'

'You can if you shoot it in the right place.'

He looked at me pleadingly. His glasses had slipped down again and the groove in his nose was like a brand mark. 'Where's the right place?'

'Between the eyes.'

He adjusted his glasses. 'You think it's the right thing to do?'

'It's the only thing.'

'I suppose you're right.'

'I'll do it,' I offered.

'You won't,' said George. 'It's my gun. I can do it myself.'

The wind came up and ripped through the leaves, and the hush that had possessed the garden was blown away. We were open to the world once more. There was no time to waste.

I held the cat firmly, trying not to hurt it, and George put the muzzle of the gun between its eyes and fired. I am certain, even now, that it felt no pain. He fired a second time. The cat shivered gigantically, and its feet traced a weary pattern in the dirt. Its legs trembled for several seconds, and it died.

'That's it,' I said.

George walked to the greenhouse, and came back with a spade. We buried the cat in a corner of the garden, and covered the grave with stones, and some sheets of corrugated iron. Neither of us said anything.

The sparrows had returned to the fence, and one or two were hopping among the pea sticks, but we left the garden and George padlocked the gate behind us. The gun was propped up against the greenhouse door, and the stock was almost luminous against the white paint.

We never shot sparrows again, and George sold the gun to a stallholder in the market for half its proper price. No-one ever asked us about the cat, and we never mentioned it again. George is foreman in his father's mill now, and I heard recently that he was getting married. We never see each other these days, and if we did there would be nothing to say.

SNAKE IN THE GRASS
by Helen Cresswell

Robin could tell, right from the beginning, that he was going to enjoy the picnic. To begin with, Uncle Joe and Auntie Joy had brought him a present, a bugle.

He took a long, testing blow. The note went on and on and on—and on. He saw Auntie Joy shudder and his cousin Nigel put his hands to his ears. Nigel was twelve, and Robin hardly even came up to his shoulder.

'We'll be off now,' Uncle Joe said, climbing into his car. 'See you there.'

Robin got into the back seat of his father's car.

'It's lovely at Miller's Beck,' his mother said. 'You'll love it, Robin.'

Robin did not reply. The picnic hamper was on the back seat, too, and he was trying to squint between the wickerwork to see what was in there. In the end he gave up squinting, and sniffed. Ham, was it? Tomatoes? Oranges, definitely, and was it—could it be—strawberries?

He sat back and began to practise the bugle. He kept playing the same three notes over and over again, and watched the back of his father's neck turning a dark red.

'D'ye *have* to play that thing now?' he growled at last. 'We shall all end up in a ditch!'

'I'm only trying to learn it, Dad,' said Robin. 'I've always wanted a bugle.'

An hour later, when they reached Miller's Beck, he had invented a tune that he really liked and had already played it about a hundred times. It was a kind of cross between Onward Christian Soldiers and My Old Man's a Dustman.

The minute the car stopped Robin got out and ran down to the stream. He pulled off his shoes and socks and paddled in. The water was icy cold and clear as tap water, running over stones and gravel and small boulders.

Robin began to paddle downstream after a piece of floating bark he wanted for a boat, when

'Ooooooooch!' he yelled. 'Owwwwch!'

A sharp pain ran through his foot. He balanced on one leg and lifted the hurt foot out of the water. He could see blood dripping from it.

'Ooooowh!' he yelled again 'Help!'

He began to sway round and round on his good leg, like a spinning top winding down. He threw out his arms, yelled again and was down, flat on his bottom in the icy beck.

'Robin' he heard his father scream. 'Robin'.

He sat where he was with the water above his waist and the hurt foot lifted above the water, still dripping blood. He couldn't even feel the foot any more. He just sat and stared at it as if it belonged to somebody else.

His father was pulling off his shoes and socks and next minute was splashing in beside him and had lifted him clean up out of the water. Robin clutched him hard and water squelched between them. Robin's elbow moved sharply and he heard his father's yell.

'Hey, my glasses.'

Robin twisted his head and saw first that he was dripping blood all over his father's trousers, second that the bottoms of his father's trousers were in the water because he hadn't had time to roll them up, and third that lying at the bottom of the beck were his father's spectacles. Robin could see at a glance that they were broken—at least, one of the lenses was.

His father staggered blindly out of the water, smack into Uncle Joe who was hopping on the bank.

'Here! Take him!' he gasped.

Then Robin was in Uncle Joe's arms, dripping blood and water all over *him*, and was carried back up the slope with his mother and Auntie Joy dancing and exclaiming around them.

It was half an hour before the picnic could really begin. By then, Robin was sitting on one of the folding chairs with his foot resting on a cushion on the other chair. This mean that both his parents were sitting on the grass. Robin's foot was bandaged with his father's handkerchief and the blood had soaked right through it and had made a great stain on the yellow cushion. Robin's shorts were hanging over the car bumper where they were dripping onto Nigel's comic, Robin was wearing his swimming trunks and had his mother's new pink cardigan draped round his shoulders. There was blood on that, too.

'*Everyone's* got a bit of blood', he noted with satisfaction.

Admittedly, his father and Uncle Joe had come off worst. His father sat half on the rug and half off with his trousers dripping. He had to keep squinting about him and twisting his head round to see through the one remaining lens of his glasses. Robin kept staring at him, thinking how queer he looked with one small, squinting eye and one familiar large one behind the thick pebble lens. It made him look a different person—more a creature than a person, really, like something come up from under the sea.

'Are you comfy, dear?' asked his mother.

Robin nodded.

'Are you hungry?'

Robin nodded.

'Ravenous.'

'Pass Robin a sandwich, Nigel!' said Auntie Joy sharply. 'Sitting there stuffing yourself! And you'd better not have any more, till we see how many Robin wants. Bless his heart! Does he look pale to you, Myra?'

The picnic got better and better every minute. Robin had at least three times his share of strawberries and Auntie Joy made Nigel give Robin his bag of crisps because she caught him sticking out his tongue at Robin. Nigel went off in a huff and found his comic all over blood and the minute he tried to turn the first page, it tore right across.

'That hankey's nearly soaked,' Robin said, watching Auntie Joy helping herself to the last of the strawberries. 'I've never seen so much blood. You should have seen it dripping into the water. It turned the whole stream a sort of horrible streaky red.'

Auntie Joy carried on spooning.

'If I'd been in the sea, I expect it'd have turned the whole *sea* red,' Robin went on. 'It was the thickest blood I ever saw. Sticky, thicky red blood—streams of it. Gallons. I bet it's killed all the fishes.'

Auntie Joy gulped and bravely spooned out the remaining juice.

'I won't bleed to death, will I?' he went on 'Bleed and bleed and bleed till there isn't another drop of blood left in my whole body, and I'm dead. Just like an empty bag, I'd be.'

Auntie Joy turned pale and put down her spoon.

'Just an empty bag of skin,' repeated Robin thoughtfully. 'That's what I'll be.'

'Of course you won't, darling!' cried his mother.

'Well, this handkerchief certainly is bloody,' said Robin. 'There must've been a bucket of blood. A *bowlful* anyway!'

Auntie Joy pushed away her bowl of strawberries.

'I wonder what it could've been?' went on Robin. 'That cut me, I mean.'

'Glass!' his mother said. 'It must have been. It's disgraceful, leaving broken glass lying about like that. Someone might have been crippled for life.'

'Dad,' said Robin, after a pause. At first his father did not hear. He had stretched out at full length and was peering closely at his newspaper with his one pebble eye.

'Dad!' His father looked up. 'Dad, hadn't you better go and pick *your* glass up? From your specs, I mean? Somebody else might go and cut themselves.'

'The child's right!' his mother cried. 'Fancy the angel thinking of that! Off you go, George, and pick it up, straight away!'

Robin's father got up slowly. His trousers flapped wetly about his legs and his bloodstained shirt clung to him.

'And mind you pick up every little bit!' she called after him, 'Don't you want those strawberries, Joy?'

She shook her head.

'Could you manage them, Robin?'

Robin could. He did. When he had finished, he licked the bowl.

Once the tea things were cleared away, everyone settled down. Auntie Joy was knitting a complicated lacy jacket that meant she had to keep counting under her breath. His mother read, Uncle Joe decided to wash his car, and his father was searching for the sports pages of his newspaper that had blown away while he was down at the beck picking up his broken spectacles. Nigel had a new model yacht and took it down to the stream. Robin watched him go. All *he* had was a sodden comic, and the bugle.

He played the bugle until the back of his father's neck was crimson again and Auntie Joy had twice lost count of her stitches and had to go right back to the beginning of the row again. For a change, he tried letting her get half way across a row and then, without warning, gave a deafening blast. She jumped, the needles jerked, and half the stitches came off.

After the third time, even that didn't seem funny any more. Robin swung his legs down and tested the bad foot. Surprisingly, it hardly hurt at all. He stood right up and took a few steps. His mother looked up.

'Robin! she squealed. 'Darling! What are you doing?'

'It's all right, Mum,' he said 'It doesn't hurt. It's stopped bleeding now. It looks worse than it is, the handkerchief being all bloody.'

'I really think you should sit still,' she said.

Robin took no notice and went limping down to the beck. Nigel was in midstream, turning his yacht. It was a beauty.

'Swap you it for my bugle,' he said, after a time.

'What?' Nigel turned to face him. 'You're crazy. Crazy little kid!'

'I'll swap,' repeated Robin.

'Well, I *won't*.' Nigel turned his back again.

Robin stayed where he was. Lying by his feet were Nigel's shoes, with the socks stuffed inside them. Gently, using the big toe of his bandaged foot, he edged them off the bank and into the water. They lay there, the shoes filled and the socks began to balloon and sway. Fascinated, Robin watched. At last the socks, with a final graceful swirl, drifted free of the shoes and began to float downstream.

Robin watched them out of sight. After that, there seemed nothing he could do. What *could* you do, with your foot all bandaged up? The picnic was going all to pieces.

He felt a little sting on his good leg and looked down in time to see a gnat making off. He swatted hard at it, and with a sudden inspiration clapped a hand to his leg, fell to his knees and let out a blood curdling howl.

'Robin!' He heard his mother scream. 'Robin!'

They were thundering down the slope towards him now, all of them, even Uncle Joe, wash leather in hand.

'Darling! what is it?'

'Snake!' gasped Robin, squeezing his leg tight with his fingers.

'Where?' cried Auntie Joy. He pointed up stream, towards the long grass. He noticed that her wool was wound round her waist and her knitting trailing behind her, both needles missing.

'Where did it *bite* you?' she cried.

Robin took his hands away from the leg. Where they had clutched it, the skin was red and in the middle of the crimson patch was the tiny prick made by the gnat.

'Oooooh!' He heard his mother give an odd, sighing moan and looked up in time to see that she was falling. His father leapt forward and caught her just in time and they both fell to the ground together.

'Biting the dust,' thought Robin, watching them.

'Here!' cried Auntie Joy. 'We'll have to suck the poison out!'

She dropped to her knees beside him, her hair awry and face flushed. Next minute she had her mouth to Robin's leg and was sucking it, with fierce, noisy sucks. He tried to jerk his leg away but she had it in an iron grip. At last she stopped sucking and turning her head aside spat fiercely right into the stream. It was almost worth having her suck, to see her spit.

'Carry him up to the car!' she gasped, scrambling up. 'I must see to Myra!'

Uncle Joe picked him up for the second time that day and carried him away. Over his shoulder Robin could see the others bending over his mother, trying to lift her. Best of all, he could see Nigel beating round in the long grass with a stick while his boat, forgotten, sailed slowly off downstream.

'Gone,' Robin thought. 'Gone for ever.'

Uncle Joe put him down in the driving seat of his own car.

'Be all right for a minute, old chap?' he asked.

Robin nodded.

'Have a mint.' He fished one from his pocket. 'Back in a minute. Better go and see if I can find that brute of a snake. Don't want Nigel bitten.'

Then he was gone. Robin stared through the windscreen towards the excited huddle by the bank. It seemed to him that everyone was having a good time except himself. There he sat, quite alone, scratching absently at the gnat bite.

Idly he looked about the inside of the car. Usually he wasn't allowed in. It was Uncle Joe's pride and joy. The dashboard glittered with knobs and dials. He twiddled one or two of them, and got the radio working, then a green light on, then a red, then the windscreen wipers working. He pushed the gearstick and it slotted smoothly into place. To his left, between the bucket seats, was the handbrake. He knew how to release it—his father had shown him.

The brake was rightly on, and it was a struggle. He was red in the face and panting by the time he sat upright again. The car was rolling forward, very gently, down the grassy slope, then gathering speed as it approached the beck.

By the time they saw him it was too late. The car lurched then bounced off the bank and into the water. It stopped, right in mid-stream.

Robin looked out and saw himself surrounded by water.

'The captain goes down with his ship!' he thought.

He saw his mother sit up, stare, then fall straight back again. He saw the others, wet, bloodstained and horrorstruck, advancing towards him.

With a sigh he let his hands fall from the wheel. It was the end of the picnic, he could see that. He wound down the window and put out a hand to wave. Instead, it met glass and warm flesh. He heard a splash and a tinkle. Level with the window, he saw his father's face. Now *both* his eyes were small and squinting. Small, squinting and murderous.

The picnic was definitely over.

DON'T TRY TO TAKE A TAXI TO COTOPAXI
by Edward Blishen

We've tried all the familiar games with pencil and paper, in my family—and have invented one or two, all of them involving rhyme. You have to be careful about this: too much of it, and rhyme becomes a sort of disease. 'I'm afraid,' says someone at breakfast, 'I need the marmalade'; to which he gets the reply, 'Hard luck! Pa has just scraped the bottom of the jar'. A whole breakfast-time of that, and someone else is saying, sharply: 'This habit of speaking in verse is becoming a positive curse!' or 'Off at once to your various schools, you poetic fools!'

So, if you play any of the games I'm going to describe, take care to play them in moderation: a half an hour at a time will do.

The first I can explain only by way of examples. It involves taking two names that can be made to have some sort of comic connection and turning them into a jingle along these lines:

Douglas
Was Jay,
But Danny
Was Kaye.

(Mr. Jay, at the time this was written, was President of the Board of Trade. Mr. Kaye needs no introduction.)

Or you could take a Liberal life peer and a famous comedian and make:

Frank
Was Byers
But Peter
Was Sellers

My favourites so far, among the jingles that have turned up during our own playing of the game, include one involving Elizabeth I's foremost statesman and a distinguished modern soldier (*William Cecil / Was Burghley / But Field Marshal Sir William / Was Slim*): the Speaker of the House of Commons and the former Secretary of State for Employment and Productivity (*Dr. The R. Hon. Horace / Was King / But Mrs. the Rt. Hon. Barbara / Was Castle*): a writer and Henry VIII's favourite wife (*Mortimer / Was Batten / But Anne / Was Boleyn*): the first four-minute miler and a great dancer (*Dr. Roger / Was Bannister / But Fred / Was Astaire*): another writer and an actor (*Monica / Was Furlong / But Sir Bernard / Was Miles*): and the father of modern science-fiction and the inventor of the sliding scale (*Jules / Was Verne / But Pierre / Was Vernier*). A useful book to have by your side is a dictionary of biography.

For the next game you need a gazetteer. With its aid you can make up four-line poems of a (usually) most irregular kind based on place-names. An example is:

The Leeward Isles
By miles and miles
Are a longer group
Than the Tonga group.

Well, that's the most regular verse we've produced. The usual shape of our gazetteer poems is like this:

Gersoppa
Is a whopper:
Or to state the fact in a way less likely to cause unseemly mirth
Gersoppa (in India) is the fourteenth largest lake on earth.

Or these:

Madagascar
Is easily distinguished from Alaska

The first is a French-speaking republic off the East African coast (or, as the French call it, côte):
The other's not.

Don't try to take a taxi
To Cotopaxi
The taxi-man is likely to say rudely: 'Why don't you fly?'
The place in question being a volcano exactly 19,613 feet high.

As a river, the Mississippi is absolutely A1,
A well-thought of and thoroughly OK one!
But it's hell
To spell

Though there's clearly nothing about Portnockie
To make the inhabitants cocky,
The reference to it in my gazetteer (which goes in for abbreviations) as a 'sm. fishing pt.'
Must make them snt.

For the last game you need simply a dictionary. The point here is to *misuse* words: that is, to use them in verse as if they had quite other meanings than those they really have. For instance, an echelon is an arrangement of troops in a step-like series, but rightly placed in a line of verse it can be made to sound like something to eat: 'He feasted on ripe echelons.' A hullabaloo is an uproar or din, but mightn't it also be a curious sort of dress: 'She wore a purple hullabaloo'? The most ambitious poem we've produced whilst playing this game runs as follows:

Amid the derringers I ride,
My graphic hat eskew:
Toupees tumble in the tide,
And the shy napkin, kapok-eyed,
Dottles the dervish dew.

The numismatic moon above
Makes sleezy all the sky;
The farad sizzles to his love;

The dermatitis and the dove
Go scapulary by.

And where the logarithm blows
Under the benzine tree,
Creatures all natty and nodose,
And balusters with buckish toes,
Run friable and free.

Oh the great mountain's gravid peak,
Tipped with the wind-blown crith,
Makes creeping carotids seem weak,
That through the high saliva sneak
And pipe their piteous pith.

When dawn breaks hispid on that hill
And all the schedules shine,
The bouillabaisse will ope its bill,
And I will mount my trusty twill
And cross from crine to crine.

Till, where the piccalilli spring,
I find a millibar:
And there my figment down I'll fling,
And tune my parasite, and sing
A sonorous raffia.

I began with a warning: I must end with one. The game with the gazetteer, I am informed by a member of my own family, can lead to guffaws in Geography. That is to say, he himself had an awkward moment or two, in class, when he had to explain—but could not—why he'd burst out laughing at the mention of, say, Woomera or Sierra Leone. An effect of playing the game too often, in fact, is that all place names begin to seem vaguely funny; and that can complicate your serious study of the atlas. As for the last game, it may gravely weaken your grasp of the true meaning of words. It can, in short, raddle you in your attempts to monster the insurrectionary. If you see what I mean.

SURPRISED
by Catherine Storr

Have you ever thought how when you think you know what something's going to be like, it turns out to be quite different? Or if it is anything like you imagined, it's somehow flat, as if you'd had it before. There may be a minute when you say, 'It's perfect, it's exactly like I imagined.' Then, another minute later, it's disappointing, just because it is how you'd imagined it. Like staying too long at a party, or thinking too much about Christmas before it comes.

My sister Tossie was always disappointed long before the end of Christmas day. She was the one of us who got most excited about Christmas; she was always awake long before we were supposed to get up on Christmas morning, waking the rest of us up too, poking at our stockings and guessing what was inside them. I remember one Christmas, she can't have been more than ten, because I know I was nearly six, it was the year we'd all had chicken-pox. She poked round a sort of long thin thing in her stocking and said, 'It's a watch.'

'It couldn't be a *watch*. It's much too expensive,' we said.

'It could. It could be a watch. What else would be that shape?'

'A pencil.'

'Too flat.'

'A bracelet.'

'Not in that shaped box.'

'A paperknife.'

'Mum wouldn't.'

We guessed all sorts of things, but Tossie wouldn't listen to any of them. She went off on a sort of dream which she told out loud, about how she'd wear the watch and how surprised her friends were going to be, and how no one except her in the upper thirds had a watch. How she'd lend it to me for parties—as long as she wasn't going to them herself, of course—and how when she was an old, old lady and died, she'd leave it to her grandchildren, with a message telling them it was the first watch she'd ever had, and she'd been given it the Christmas she was ten.

It turned out to be a pair of compasses, something she'd always wanted before, but of course not like having a proper watch. That was another sad Christmas. Somehow when Tossie was sad it made us all feel as if we'd been disappointed about our presents too. Our Mum used to say she built up such a rigmarole in her head about how marvellous everything was going to be that nothing, not watches or bicycles or diamond rings or the Queen's crown could have come up to what she'd imagined. And it was always like that. She'd come back sad from parties, because each one was going to be the most marvellous party she'd ever been to; then when it turned out to be just being with the same lot of people she'd seen every day at school all term, but wearing different clothes and not having anything special to do, she felt let down and awful. I used to dread Tossie's parties because of her and me sharing the room. I'd be asleep when she came in, but when it had been a bad evening she wouldn't bother about being quiet. She'd drop her shoes, shut the wardrobe door so it slammed as well as squeaked—which you couldn't help—and then lie in bed sighing. Tossie had the biggest sighs I've ever heard, it was like hearing a hippopotamus feeling sad. Sometimes I'd say, 'Tossie?'

'What?' she'd say, sounding cross, though she wasn't.

'Was the party fun?'

'No.'

'Tell.'

'Nothing to tell.'

'What happened?'

'Nothing happened.'

'Didn't they like your dress?'

'No one said.'

'What did you do?'

'Nothing.'

'Did you meet any boys?' I knew it was risky asking this, but I generally couldn't stop myself.

'I suppose so.'

If I was feeling brave I'd go one step further.

'Did any of them try to kiss you?'

'Go to sleep. It's long past your bedtime.'

But I couldn't get to sleep until Tossie had stopped those awful deep sighs, and the restless turning in bed. Even that wasn't the worst, though. The worst was when I heard her sniffing into the pillow. I didn't feel better about this until one morning when I heard Tossie tell Mum that she'd cried till her pillow was wet with tears. So at least one of Tossie's imaginings had been made to come true.

When Tossie started going with boys, I mean really, not just seeing them gooping at the parties, but having them call for her and taking her out to coffee bars, I knew we had a bad time coming. When I said this to Mum she said not to be a something or other.

'What's that?'

'Jeremiah. Sad sort of chap, always saw bad things coming.'

'Am I? I mean, do I?'

'Not more than most, I daresay. Still, you and Tossie, you are a pair.'

'I see things the way they are. Tossie sees them how she wants them to be.'

Mum said, 'Well, I don't know.' She often said that, but I thought she knew quite a lot, really.

As it turned out, Tossie's love affairs weren't so much awful as wearing. That isn't quite true, because the first few were awful. Then I got used to the way they happened. In fact I got so used, I could almost tell when the next stage was due. They went like this. First of all Tossie would go very quiet and mysterious. If you said anything to her, she'd sort of come back to earth with a start, as if she'd been miles away. If you asked, she'd say no, she wasn't thinking about anything in particular, smiling all the time a secret smile that meant just the opposite of what she said. This was while she and the boy were sort of eyeing each other, they hadn't said anything yet. Then when he'd come out with saying he was crazy about her, or whatever it was, and they'd kissed a bit, Tossie couldn't talk about anything else. As far as I can remember, with the first one or two, or perhaps three, I really did think, 'This is it. Tossie's going to marry John (or perhaps it was Martin or David or Joe) 'she'll be a bride at sixteen, I'll be an aunt before I take my "O" levels.' It would be a marvellous time—it got boring later—with Tossie on top of the world, telling us how tremendous John (or Martin or David) was, and how she'd never felt like this before, how it was all that love was written up to be, and better. She'd keep me awake late into the night, talking about whichever it was, how she loved him, how he loved her, how clever he was, how they must have been meant for each other, the lot. Of course when she got on to the later ones there'd be a lot of comparing: How John had really been too changeable, she could see that now, and how she'd wondered at the time if Martin was a strong enough character for her, and how David had been slow in the uptake, but how now Joe . . .

Then there'd come the time that was like opening the stocking and finding it wasn't a watch after all. First of all she'd be home evenings when we'd thought she'd be out, sometimes explaining, sometimes not. Then she'd be very touchy; you couldn't say anything without having your head bitten off. After a bit of this, there'd be a night when she'd keep me awake gulping and sighing, even groaning sometimes, saying things in between like, 'Don't ever fall in love Barb, it's bloody hell,' (her language always got a bit lurid at these times), or 'I know now, everything they say about not trusting men is true.' After a week or so of this, with Tossie going around looking like Ophelia and The Lady of the Camellias rolled into one (a lot of eyeshadow, and I swear that even Mum got worried once or twice about the cough she used to get at these times) she'd begin to recover. First of all she'd be a brave little woman who was going to bury herself in her work (it was a tremendous piece of luck that she had a month just before her 'A' levels in between Sammy and Dan) and then, sometimes gradually, sometimes suddenly, it would begin all over again. She'd forget her career and it would be all romance. She had a bottom drawer she put things into when she got something new and pretty. The trouble was it went through off seasons like Tossie's love life, and when she was going to be a career woman she'd take out the new nylon nightie she'd put there for her wedding to John/Martin/David/Joe, etc. and she'd wear it, enjoying herself, in a way, doing it and suffering. She talked a lot about suffering during this time.

She'd get me worried sometimes, thinking that whatever happened to Tossie was, of course, going to happen to me as soon as I was old enough. For me, you see, it was almost like having a crystal ball showing me what my life would be like in a year or so, and though I wanted this business of being in love and going out with boys and everything, I didn't want to suffer. Or at least, not like Tossie did.

I think I'm sounding rather bitchy about Tossie and her sufferings, but this really isn't fair. She certainly did suffer. The trouble is that when you share a room with someone who suffers such a lot you sort of get used to it. You even get a bit bored.

I can't remember now how long Tossie went on like that. It was probably quite a time, because I know that I'd got to that sort of stage myself, where I was wondering all the time when some boy would want to take me out, and feeling sure none of them ever would. So perhaps I didn't notice so much about Tossie: or it may have been that if something goes on long enough, you don't notice all at once if it stops. Like a headache. You suddenly realise you haven't been noticing it for the last quarter of an hour, which means that it's gone. I suddenly noticed about Tossie that way. Not that she'd gone, but that she was different.

I said before how at the beginning of a new boy she'd go quiet; but it never lasted. What I realised this time was that she'd been quiet for ever so long.

I would have said it wasn't natural, only that she didn't feel unnatural. She was kind of peaceful, and yet it wasn't peaceful like being asleep. It was more like waiting. Even that's not quite right, because it wasn't like waiting for something you're worried about, not like that feeling that you *can't* wait it's so exciting, like a birthday or a party or a match. More like waiting for something to grow, like mustard and cress on a flannel in a saucer, where you notice each leaf as it comes out, and it almost doesn't matter when you eat it, because the growing it's been exciting too.

But it wasn't like Tossie. It wasn't like her to wait that way. It wasn't like her not to have to talk about it. I could see she wasn't unhappy, either. Every night she was out, and every night she'd come in so quietly I never woke up. There wasn't any sighing and groaning. I couldn't understand it. It was funny. Different.

At last I said to her, 'Tossie. What's going on?'

'What's going on?' she said back.

'It isn't Jamie, is it?' I knew it wasn't really. Jamie had been weeks back.

'Jamie and I broke up seven weeks and two days ago.'

I saw then what a long time I'd taken to catch on. And I was interested she'd got it so exact too, Tossie being apt to exaggerate a lot.

'What's up, then, Toss?'

She said, 'I don't really know.'

Now that was the first time I'd heard my sister Tossie admit she didn't know what was up.

'Is it Barry, Tossie?' Barry was the fellow she'd been going out with lately.

' 'Course it's Barry.'

'Is he crazy about you?'

'I don't know,' she said again.

'Are you in love with him?'

This time, when she said, 'I don't know,' again, she really shook me. I'd been a bit drowsy before, but that really woke me up with a jolt.

'But Tossie, you must know. You've been in love before.'

'I'm not sure I have,' she said.

I thought about this.

'What does it feel like, then?' I asked.

She said, 'Barb, it's different.'

'Well, do you love him?' I asked.

'He's not the sort of boy I generally go for,' she said.

'Go on.'

'I sort of can't help liking him. You know. I like him being around. I feel sort of . . .'

'Sort of what?'

'Comfortable. When he's there.'

'Not in love, then?' I said, disappointed.

'I don't know.'

Tossie seemed to me, by this time, so experienced I couldn't understand how it was she didn't know if she was in love or not. I said, 'Well, what then?'

She said, slowly, 'Perhaps I am. P'raps this is what it's really like. Not like anything you thought it would be.'

'What then?' I asked again wanting to know, so I'd be able to tell when it happened to me.

Tossie said, 'Surprised. All the time I don't feel like what I thought I would. I'm always being surprised.'

THE SEAFARING OF KARI ASMUNDSON
by Jill Paton-Walsh

There was a man called Kari Asmundson, who lived at Upfell on Koningsfiord. Kari had extensive lands, and a fine house, and he owned a ship, in which he used to go voyaging one summer in two. He was a thoroughly respected man. Sometimes his neighbours would come and consult him on a voyage they were making, or ask his advice about a law-suit. In spite of this he was not well-liked, for he was inclined to be stubborn and surly, and had a long memory for small grievances. Kari was married to Jorunn Hild's daughter, who was half-sister to Einar Ragnasson, who lived at Ragnastead on the other side of Upfell from Kari's farm.

Kari went on a voyage, leaving Jorunn to look after his affairs in Norway. Jorunn was a capable woman, thrifty, and well respected in the district. She was devoted to Einar, her half-brother, and would usually do anything he asked of her. Einar had a brother called Mork who lived with him at Ragnastead. Mork was the son of a slave-woman, and no relation at all to Jorunn. It happened that Einar's sheep had strayed, and he sent Mork to Jorunn to ask for her help. The sheep had wandered all over Upfell, and Einar had not enough men to round them up. Mork found Jorunn in Kari's hayfield, helping to bind the ricks. He told Jorunn why he had come.

'I will send help tomorrow, when my field is cut,' said Jorunn.

'Many of Einar's sheep will have fallen from the cliffs into the sea by then,' said Mork. 'But your hayfield will not have moved.'

'Very well, then,' said Jorunn. She sent her men across Upfell to help Einar, and they did not return till nightfall. In the night a storm broke, and the hay was beaten down and soaked with rain so that most of it was ruined. Jorunn thought it likely that Kari would have to spend the profit from his voyage buying hay from his neighbours that winter.

Shortly after Kari came home he rode over to Ragnastead to see Einar. Einar made Kari welcome, and asked for news of his voyage.

'We will talk of that later, when we have agreed what compensation you will pay me for causing the loss of my hay,' said Kari.

'It is bad luck that a storm should spoil your hay,' said Einar. 'But it is certainly no doing of mine. As for Jorunn lending me a few of your men, that is only the sort of thing than any man does for his neighbours.'

'I do not see matters in that light at all,' said Kari. 'But time will put it to the test.' With that he left Olafstead.

'I doubt if Kari's voyaging has made him much profit this year,' said Mork to Einar.

The winter came early and was exceptionally severe that year. Kari's livestock suffered greatly from the lack of hay in his barns, and he was obliged to kill off many of his sheep. He brooded over his injury, and was sullen with Jorunn because of the favour she had done to Einar. Then when the snow was very heavy he summoned his servant, Thord. 'Go to Ragnastead, and ask Einar to lend me some of his men,' he said. 'Tell him that the roof of my barn is sagging under the weight of snowfall, and I have not men enough to bring timber down from the wood and prop it up.'

Jorunn was crossing the yard. 'The roof of the barn looks straight enough to me,' she said.

The snow was so thick on Upfell that Thord had a hard journey, and it was nearly night by the time he reached Ragnastead.

'You may sleep in the byre tonight, and return to Kari in the morning,' said Einar. 'As for sending help to him, you can see for yourself that it would not reach him before nightfall tomorrow. If Kari's barn has not fallen down by tomorrow night, it will doubtless stand up till the thaw.'

'As soon as the ice melts in the fiord, I am going on another journey,' Kari told Jorunn. 'Things are in a bad way, and I shall need to make money by some means.'

'What had you in mind?' asked Jorunn.

'They say King Olaf is keeping several important, and other Icelanders hostages, till the Icelanders accept the Christ-god,' said Kari. 'I will fell trees on Upfell, and take timber to Iceland for church building. And you had better take more care than you did last time I was away. There is bad feeling now between Einar and me, and if anything worsens it, I will not answer for what may happen.'

'As to that,' said Jorunn, 'Einar is going abroad in the spring as well as you.'

Kari was not the only one who had thought of a need for timber in Iceland. Before the ice broke up on the fiord friends had brought word to him that Starkad Grimson was loading timber, and making his ship ready for the thaw.

When the ice broke up in the spring the wind veered and blew again from the north. Three weeks after the ice breaking there were still ice floes floating in the water, keeping the ships in the fiord. Friends brought word to Kari that Starkad Grimson was putting to sea, hoping to steer through the ice floes into open water.

'The first comer will get the best price for his wares,' said Kari, 'and it will not be Starkad Grimson.' Then he ran his ship down into the water, and began to row towards the sea. There were ice floes bobbing in the water either side of the ship, and the wind still blowing from the north. Then one of Kari's men saw Starkad's ship, coming down the fiord some way behind them.

'I have been cheated once too often by my neighbours,' said Kari. 'Run up the sail.'

'That is too risky, Kari,' said Thord, who was sailing with him. 'Do as I say,' said Kari.

Kari sailed down Koningsfiord towards the sea, with Starkad behind him. He avoided striking any ice floes. Then they came to the sea, and the ice was floating there too. They could see that there were three ships putting out from Ragnafiord, on their steering side, under sail, and some way ahead.

At that moment they were struck by a violent squall. Kari's men ran down the sail just in time. Hailstones rattled on the ship, and sea spume lashed into her. Nothing could be seen. Kari was afraid of striking ice, but his good luck held.

When the storm had passed Kari could see no other ships. He set sail again on the same course as before. After a while they came upon wreckage, drifting in the sea. Then Kari knew that the ships from Ragnafiord had perished in the storm.

'There is an ice floe ahead of us, Kari,' said Thord.

'Steer to the north of it,' said Kari. By this time they could see a man clinging to the floe.

'There is a man from Ragnafiord,' said Thord. 'Shall we lower the sails?'

'No,' said Kari. 'The man I see is Einar Ragnason, who has delayed an enterprise of mine once before. He will have got the better of me again if because of him Starkad overtakes me.'

When Einar Ragnasson saw Kari's ship he was overjoyed at first. He could not believe that Kari would not stop for him. As Kari's ship came on, still going fast, under sail, Einar began to shout. Then he let go of the ice floe, and swam towards Kari, calling him. Kari did not answer, and his ship left Einar far behind. Then Einar Ragnasson swallowed sea-water, and sank.

Kari made a landfall in the Orkneys. Nothing further of any consequence happened on the journey. When the ship was at Stromness, Kari sent Thord to buy new rope and new oars to make good the damage done by the storm. While Thord was away Kari's men came to him.

'We cannot sail with you again, Kari,' they said. 'Your ship is followed everywhere by a man swimming in the wake, and calling, "Kari, Kari!" '

'You are drunk!' said Kari. 'I did not see that. Anyway, until I sell my timber, I cannot pay you. You must sail with me till then, or go unpaid.'

'We will go unpaid,' they said.

When Thord came back Kari said, 'Come Thord. We must cross at once to another of these islands, to raise a crew before the news of our bad luck can go before us.' Kari sat on the rowing bench beside Thord, and the two men laboured to row the boat out of the haven, and into the wind. Then they sailed to Hoy.

At Hoy, Kari raised a new crew, promising to pay well, and return them to Hoy on the homeward journey. Then he sailed to Faeroe, and made a landfall in three days sailing. At Faeroe he landed at Thorshaven, to pick up fresh water, but no sooner had his ship touched land than the men of Hoy came to him and said, 'We sail no further with you, Kari. Your ship is full of dreams.'

'What do you mean?' asked Kari. He was greatly disturbed.

'These three days and nights we have dreamed of a man swimming in your wake, Kari, and we will sail with you no more.'

'What of my promise, that I would take you home when my timber was sold?' asked Kari.

'As to that, we will get home as best we may,' they said.

'Come Thord,' said Kari. 'We must find a new crew swiftly, before news of our luck can travel.' Kari and Thord crossed over to another island, and there found another crew, and set sail in haste. Kari sailed to Iceland, and made a landfall in three days sailing. As soon as Kari's ship was beached at Esjuberg in Hvalfiord his men came to him, and said they would not sail home with him.

'There will be other ships going to the Faeroes,' they said.

'There will also be mine,' said Kari.

'There are dreams in your ship,' said the Faeroe men, 'and a voice calling your name that grows fainter and fainter, but never dies out of earshot.'

'It has happened again,' said Kari to Thord.

'I too have seen Einar following us,' said Thord. 'It seems to me you need help, Kari.'

'Who can help me in such an affair as this?' said Kari.

'I have heard of an Icelander called Njal Thorgeirsson who can see into the future,' said Thord. 'Perhaps he would know what you must do.'

Njal Thorgeirsson lived at Bergthorsknoll, two days ride to the south. He made Kari welcome, and offered him food and drink.

'There is a ghost which follows my ship,' Kari told him, 'so that I cannot get men to sail with me.'

Njal said nothing for a long time. 'When I think of this,' he said at last, 'I see a coast where two fiords run out to the sea, and there is a high craggy hill between them. Do you know this place?"

'I know it,' said Kari.

'For as long as you sail away from this place the evil you have done will follow you,' said Njal. 'You must return there.' Kari thanked Njal, and gave him a present of a woollen cloak he had brought with him from Norway.

Kari sold all his timber at a good price, although as it happened Starkad Grimsson had reached Iceland before him.

Kari had difficulty finding a crew for the journey homeward. The men from Faeroe had been talking, and it seemed that everyone in Iceland had heard of the dream's on Kari's ship. After a while, however, he found enough men to sail. They were morose, not liking the prospect before them. Most of them had their own reasons for taking a passage out of Iceland in a hurry, and some of the reasons were pressing enough.

Nothing of any consequence happened on the journey, until the coast of Norway came in sight. Kari could see Upfell, and the mouth of Ragnafiord on one side, and Koningsfiord on the other, just as it had appeared to Njal Thorgeirsson.

'Steer for Koningsfiord,' Kari told Thord.

At that moment a harsh wind began to blow, and a great wave came up on the steering side, and rolled the ship over. Kari found himself swimming. The wave and the wind had together disappeared, and the ship was floating upside down a little way off. There was no sign of any of Kari's companions.

Kari swam to his boat, and scrambled up till he could sit astride the keel. He sat there for the rest of the day, and all night, and all the following night, until his strength was almost exhausted. When the dawn broke Kari began to see visions. He thought he saw Einar Ragnasson swimming up to his boat, and trying to climb onto it. Then he looked again, and saw that he had seen the body of Thord, floating face downwards, a little way behind the ship. He thought he saw the coastline coming nearer and nearer, as though the ship were drifting rapidly ashore; then he looked again and saw the coast just as far off as before, and still too far to swim. He heard tapping on the upturned boat; men trapped underneath it, frantically tapping to get out. It was only driftwood, knocking on the hull in the wash of the sea. Then he saw a sea-monster, swimming alongside. He rubbed at his eyes, and saw only the scaly sheen on the serpentine rucking of the waves.

'Who would have thought my mind would give out before my arms?' said Kari.

Then Kari saw ships. He looked again and again, and still he saw them. The light of the morning brightened as the sun came up behind Upfell, and still Kari saw ships—four ships, putting out from Ragnafiord, and sailing towards him.

When he was sure the ships were not part of his madness, Kari was overjoyed. The first ship came on under sail, and went straight past him, although he called out as loudly as he could.

'Curs!' yelled Kari after it. 'Haven't I waited here long enough? Ill-luck seize you!' Then he waited for the second ship, waving his swollen arms, and calling across the water. But the second ship also passed him by.

'Swine!' Kari called after it. 'May Thor sink your ship! May you all fall sick, and drift for days till you die!' Then the third ship was upon him. This ship sailed so near Kari, that he could see the faces of the men aboard her, but they all looked ahead, and not at him, and Kari's voice was so hoarse and feeble that he could not reach them.

'Thor! Or the White Christ!' cried Kari, 'Whichever god is in charge of things nowadays, look what these bastards are doing to me! May worm rot the timbers of their ship, may they sink, may they die, may they die the long death from thirst in the deserts of salt water!'

Now the last ship was sailing towards him. And Kari knew from the pennant at the mast-head that this ship belonged to Mork, Einar's brother from Ragnastead.

'How little I care for a load of hay now,' said Kari, groaning. Then, when Mork's ship sailed past him, Kari bowed down his head, and wept. 'Einar,' he murmured, 'Einar, my brother.'

While Kari leaned down and wept, Mork, looking back on the wake of his ship towards Upfell, saw him. He gave his men orders to run down the sail at once, and row back to the shipwrecked man.

Mork took Kari to England, where he waited a month for a ship to take him home. He did not arrive destitute, for the money from the cargo of timber had been sewn into his shirt. Nevertheless, Jorunn would not live with him after that. She went to Einar's empty house at Ragnastead, and farmed there till she was an old woman. Mork brought a law-suit against her on his return, saying that the farm belonged to him, but the case was decided against him.

Kari sold his farm, and went to Oslo, where King Olaf was building a great church. Kari became a priest there, and said prayers for Einar Ragnasson, to this god or to that, day by day until he died.

POP
by Tom Hutchinson

The father of Simon Storm greeted me at the door of the theatre dressing room with a handshake so fervent and sincere I might just have recovered from a near-fatal illness. 'It's good of you to come and see Simon,' he said. 'I've always had a great respect for your paper.' It always surprised me when people said this about the newspaper I worked for, but they did go on saying it. Perhaps they had been conditioned to be at home and in comfort among the black violence of the headlines.

Simon Storm's father led me into the room and I sat down. 'Simon's still on the stage,' he said. 'He's going down great. Just great.' He put up his hand in an almost religious gesture. 'Listen.'

We listened. As in most dressing rooms there was a one-way loudspeaker, a grilled box, linking us to the illusion being built up out there on the stage. You could hear Simon singing. Occasionally, a girl's scream of ecstasy drilled through the opaque mass of sound that he and his backing group were creating. He was obviously gyrating his body again, fulfilling his audience, countering their mass affection with a physical poignancy that was very much his own.

'Isn't he great?' asked the father of Simon Storm.

'Marvellous,' I said.

I had seen Simon's act many times. Of its kind it was competent, good even. His voice had a raucous sexuality that was nearly as much his own as derived from the hundreds of records of American blues singers he had collected over the years. He was seventeen now, old in his kind of experience, and you could hardly tell where imitation fell away and the real Simon Storm took over.

It did not matter, anyway, to the millions of fans who paid out their money to buy a dream of Simon Storm, the Simon they had created in their own image. Simon singing for them. Simon loving them. Their Simon.

In a way he was rather old-fashioned, a hangover from the days when Rock was a simple love affair between a solo artist and his audience, the days when Elvis and Cliff and Tommy had gone on lone safari into the jungle of teenagers' fantasies and come back with a Top Ten trophy and money enough to plug up any holes in the heart.

That was before the groups massed and attacked: the new generation of sophisticates knowing all about Stockhausen and Bach as well as work-songs and Ellington. To these—and they had told me—Simon was pure corn.

He still survived, though, proving something or other about our pop-culture which the tame psychologist on my paper was always trying to pin down in words of one syllable.

'It's about this series,' I said to the father. 'We fixed it up with Mr. Berg. That tour of the States.'

'Yes, yes. Mr. Berg told us.' His eyes flickered up to the huge photograph of Simon alongside the dressing-table looking glass. I realised it was for some kind of reassurance and I wondered why. Other pictures—of The Beatles, The Rolling Stones, The Who—stared down at us.

Simon, alone, seemed vulnerable. Blond, blue-eyed, his thin body as taut as a rabbit in a trap. I supposed this was what his fans liked about him, recognising something in him of themselves. It never came through to me, but then *I* liked Frank Sinatra.

'You're going to America with us,' the father went on. 'Mr. Berg told us. To write up the tour, how big Simon goes down over there. You can discuss it with me, all right. Ever since Simon's mother died I've been mother *and* father to Simon.' He smiled proudly. 'Mr. Berg says I'm as good as any manager.'

Suddenly I liked Simon Storm's father, for that pride and for the innocence in that pride.

He was a dumpling little man with a Midlands voice, sounding as though it were slightly choked with soot; you kept wanting to clear his throat for him. His eyes were sad little pools of watery blue. His waistcoat was buttoned up so tightly it looked uncomfortable, but he looked right in its beatle-sheathing.

I thought that I had better get the worst over with. 'Of course,' I said, 'we'd want to mention the drugs . . . how Simon is off them now. A sort of lesson for all those youngsters who worship him. They'd see how marvellous Simon has been in shaking the habit.'

He had his back to me and was pouring a drink. His voice was suddenly shredded thin and bleak. 'Do we have to?'

I didn't want any trouble from the father; Mr. Berg had told me that convincing him was more than half the battle. I settled myself into the faded green armchair and waged war. 'Mr. Berg agreed,' I said with heavy emphasis. We both knew who the real mother and father was of Simon's act.

The father sat down. 'Mr. Berg's been very good to us. He saw the future in Simon when no other agent would give him an audition. I wouldn't want to go against Mr. Berg. But . . .'

'Come on,' I said. 'It's good publicity in a way. It proves Simon's strength by telling how he overcame weakness'—I liked that line—'it shows how he can fight temptation. Nobody wants a hero without faults these days.'

He looked at me, his face stiff with surprise. 'I never looked at it that way. It was just something rotten in the life that Simon and I share together. We had to fight it together as well Simon went through hell to kick the habit. To talk about something so private would be . . . wrong.'

'But everybody knows about it.'

'Only the people in the business. Not them out there.' He waved a slack hand in the direction of the loudspeaker where applause surged like the sea. 'He's still their idol.'

I let silence grow up around the two of us and when it was too obviously an embarrassment I said, 'How did it start?'

'I don't know, really. I used to blame myself for pushing him too hard, but Simon enjoys the business, so I don't see how it could have been my fault. He's a real trouper, you know. Always on time for rehearsals, no temperament. A real professional. . . . How well do you know him?'

'Hardly at all,' I said. I meant it. I had interviewed Simon a few times, but merely glanced off the flip façade that he erected, under Mr. Berg's tuition, for journalists.

'He's very quiet really. Like his mother used to be. She was a quiet one. She'd rather sit and knit at home than go out with me, when I used to go singing at the concerts in the local clubs at home.'

'Singing's in the family then,' I said, using the cliché hopefully, to lever him open some more.

'Not like Simon. I was just a ballad singer who'd earn a few bob at night when I'd finished at the office. I wasn't an artist the way Simon is.' He laughed as though he were hearing what he had to say for the first time, when I felt that he had said it often before. 'I used to sing for my supper.'

'And Simon?'

'He used to sing all the time around the house. He happened to us, you know, rather late in life, so my wife and I never complained about the noise; he was our only child. When my wife died Simon was four years old. Of course, he didn't really know what had happened. I remember he sang softly all the way through the funeral service, while I held his hand. It was a pop song, "Rock Around The Clock." '

It was becoming maudlin. 'Better than "Rock Of Ages," ' I said. 'Although not as appropriate.'

He went on as though I hadn't said anything, as of course I hadn't.

'I brought in a housekeeper to look after him during the day because I wasn't going to let him go to anyone else away from me. I stopped the concerts because that meant I couldn't tuck him up at night. He would have missed that. We got on well together.'

'He always liked singing?'

'And listening to singing. I bought him a record-player when he was seven and he'd use his pocket-money to buy record after record. I supposed I spoiled him. He used to sing very loudly to those records, even though he was quiet in himself. I knew he had talent then, even a potential. I didn't know how big until Mr. Berg told me.'

'That was when he was fourteen?'

'That's right. Simon had gone in for one of those amateur shows on television. I didn't like the quiz master, he was so rude to the audience when the cameras weren't on. I don't think they realised he was insulting them, but I did. Anyway, he was nice to Simon and Simon got third prize in a nation-wide poll. That quiz-master now says that he got Simon into the big-time.'

'But it was Mr. Berg.'

'Yes we met Mr. Berg. He has a tremendous personality, you know. He talked about the future and Tin Pan Alley and exclusive percentages and the like. But, underneath all that slick talk I could see he was honest and I knew he would be right for Simon.'

'Shrewd of you,' I said, thinking of Mr. Berg, so knowing about small print and big fees. He was a pusher all right, known for his stable of young singers. A friend who knew him well said, 'Berg promises these kids the moon and gives them mouldy cheese instead.'

'Mr. Berg is very skilful,' I said.

'Oh, yes. He was really the one who set up Simon's act. He taught him how to move his body in rhythm to the song, how to project his personality.

'He insisted on discipline. Regular rehearsals. On time; that sort of thing. Somebody—not from your paper—said that Simon was a puppet on a string and that worried Simon for days. But, as I pointed out, Mr. Berg was fighting for him. You have to fight.'

'And Mr. Berg wasn't fighting for himself?' It was the kind of question that I shouldn't have asked; it could have destroyed the relationship we had built up, Simon Storm's father and myself. I had to stop doing it, seeing things objectively.

'Oh, I know Mr. Berg made, is making, money out of Simon. That's business. But what he did was right for Simon. I could see that and so, eventually, did Simon. Rehearsals, rehearsals, rehearsals. Every note tuned to the right pitch. Sometimes, watching him, I didn't recognise my own child. He had become a star.'

'And the drugs?' I asked gently.

It was the right thing to say. You get an instinct for that sort of thing if you interview enough people. My question merely propelled him further along the confessional road. It didn't throw him at all. Perhaps his words walked more carefully over what he was saying, in case he fell into any cracks in the pavement.

'I got worried when Simon started being sick in the mornings and when his eyes used to glaze over sometimes. He'd be happy one minute and the next he'd be shouting and using words I didn't know he knew, hurtful words at me, his father. Mr. Berg spotted it; he knew what it was all about. He's a man of wide experience and he'd seen it before.

'As you know, as people know in the business, it was only a mild case of drug addiction. Just pills; he hadn't been injecting. Berg said there was only one solution and that was for Simon to go into this home for a couple of months.'

I was intrigued. 'What about the authorities? I thought there were regulations for minors in the theatre.'

'I don't really know'—he was puffing slightly as though he had run a long way—'nobody made any fuss. Simon went away for a while and it was thought best that I didn't see him or visit him.'

'Quite a wrench for you,' I said.

Simon Storm's father looked back and was appalled. 'Horrifying. But worse for Simon. He used to write me dreadful letters, blaming me for everything. I can't begin to tell you. But he was all right when he came out. He said ,"I've kicked it now, Pop. I'm on the up-beat again. I'm going to work." And he's done that ever since: work, work, work. He's never tired. And he relies on me now more than ever: as dresser, as manager, as friend.'

'And now the trip to the States?'

'That's essential. I can see that. The Beatles did it after all. Simon really becomes international there. That's where it's all at.' He sounded as though he was quoting somebody, possibly Mr. Berg.

'That's where I think mentioning the drugs would help,' I said. 'To be completely ruthless—and you're a man of the world and will understand—I think that kind of disclosure would generate the kind of sympathy we're after. It would help his image a good deal.'

I put a lot into those words. I knew just how much my paper—the paper that Simon's father respected so much—had paid Mr. Berg for the exclusive rights to the story. I knew how much I was paid.

He sighed, 'I suppose you're right. It's really for Simon to decide, but I can see what you mean. It's so difficult in this business to know whether you're doing the right thing. You feel that you're being got at and manipulated. But I know it's wrong to feel this way. After all the business has been good to us: it's bought Simon a lot of the things that I wouldn't normally have been able to afford for him.'

I knew then I had won.

'I think you're doing the right thing,' I said.

He relaxed. And looked naïvely sly. 'You know, for a journalist you never asked the one question they all ask.'

'Which is?'

'Simon's real name.'

I suppose in the world of Lear Tempest and Flash Lightning I should have thought of that one.

I laughed. 'Sir,' I said. 'Is Simon's real name Storm?'

He looked delighted. 'As a matter of fact it is. I am Robert Storm and Simon is Simon Storm. That's our real name. We are real people.'

He went on talking and, bored, I listened. You're often treated as a tape recorder by the people you interview; you console yourself by knowing how you will interpret the playback. On the loudspeaker Simon was singing about 'Love' in a way that made me realise just how much the real emotion had leaked away from us in this day and age; he sang about it as though it were still relevant.

The loudspeaker suddenly cracked almost wide open with noise and it was hard to identify the sound, but I worked it out. It was final applause; affection made manifest. Simon Storm had finished.

I stood up to greet him as he came off stage. Along the corridor outside I could hear the coming clatter of him, the applause trailing behind him like the hem of a distant garment.

Simon's father sat where he was as Simon came nearer. 'I'm sure it'll be all right,' he said softly. 'Mentioning the drugs, I mean. But we'll let Simon decide.'

Then he, too, stood up as the door opened and he looked upon his son. Robert Storm's face was bright in the reflected light from the corridor. I noticed all this in passing because, hand outstretched, I was already greeting Simon Storm.

'You were great,' I said.

STRANGE FISH
by Leon Garfield

The signpost's battered finger pointed towards the sea as if it was accusing it of something disagreeable. A man and youth, breathing heavily from the effort of walking over rough ground, stared at it in silence.

'What do you say?' asked the man at length. The youth squinted up. He was about fifteen, sturdy and with humorous eyes already well-crinkled from sun and sea. 'One mile to somewhere, pa,' he said. 'All that's left is Saint; but Saint what, the Lord knows. It's gone with the weather.'

The man grunted and clapped his great roughened hand about his son's shoulder as if congratulating him on his scholarship. Then they trudged on through the cold November sunshine to the village that had lost its name. It lay in the crook of a narrow bay—a quiet huddle of stone cottages with an old church standing a little way apart as if it had taken offence, perhaps on account of the forgotten saint. Indeed, the air of reproach seemed to hang pretty heavily over the whole village and even over the bay where the bright sea sighed and dragged as if it longed to take itself off elsewhere. There was only one boat on the beach and no nets to be seen; but this was not surprising as the weather was fair. The father and son halted again and stared out to sea for a glimpse of fishermen; but the lowering sun was bright on the water and no amount of eye-shading or squinting could distinguish anything for certain so they continued down the rough path that dropped away between tufted hillocks that here and there rose shoulder high. Suddenly the youth clutched his face and gave a cry of anger and pain.

'What is it, Sammy? Fly?' 'Stone, pa. Someone threw a stone.' He scrambled up the bank with his father following and, crouching in the long grass some five yards off, saw the first signs of life from the quiet village. Three children, supernaturally ragged and dirty. They were about five years old, one boy and two girls; but which of them had thrown the stone was impossible to say. They all looked as savage and hostile as each other.

'Where's your pa?' asked Sam, rubbing his cheek and scowling threateningly. The boy stood up and pointed towards the church. 'And yours?' he asked the girls, who looked to be no relation. They glanced at their companion and climbed to their feet. They too pointed towards the church.

'It ain't Sunday, is it, Sammy?' asked his father, who'd lost count of the days during their journey across country. Sam turned to answer that to the best of his belief it was a Tuesday, when the three venomous children took advantage of the distraction and fled. They had not uttered a single word, either to Sam and his father, or to each other. They might have been malignant spirits who'd vanished into the air.

Nonetheless the man and youth turned their steps towards the church, though with no great hopes. God-fearing though the village might have been, Tuesday afternoon was an unnatural time to be in church.

Sure enough, the church was deserted. Empty pews gazed at the empty altar, and a roughly made ship's model that hung in the doorway cast its shadow across the aisle, where it swayed and foundered among the shadows of the pew backs.

Puzzled and angry, they went outside again resolved to knock up the nearest cottage, holy Tuesday or no, when Sam pointed to the churchyard that lay beyond the church's western wall. Aged stones leaned among the tall grass, peering and peeping as if striving to read each other's inscriptions. But past this tumbled, crumbling part was another, very neat and green. It looked almost like a great gown laid out to dry and fixed with pegs and stone.

Curiously the father and son walked towards it; for it was an odd, almost uncanny sight . . . the graves being so neatly laid as if a small regiment had perished on parade and been buried where they'd stood.

'What do they say, Sammy?' muttered his father. 'You know I come without me spectacles.'

Sam nodded. Though his father had a pair of spectacles which he'd found in the cabin of a wreck; and though he often wore them of an evening by the fire, they were more of a personal ornament than anything else as he was quite unable to read. He never admitted this weakness to his wife or son (though they knew it perfectly well), not because he was ashamed but because he was the head of the house and it was against nature for a woman or a boy to be more proficient than he. So when there was any reading to be done, his spectacles were more useful in their absence than on his nose, where they only served to hide the marvellous brightness of his eyes.

'Jacob Tulliver,' read Sam from the nearest stone. 'Taken November seven, 1749. Rest in Peace.'

'Only a year in his grave,' murmured Sam's father. 'And the grass as thick as a cushion.'

'John Blazey,' continued Sam, from the next stone. 'Taken November seven, 1749. Rest in Peace.' He frowned, then moved on. 'Ezra Till. Taken November seven, 1749. Rest in Peace.'

'What? Three of 'em on the same day? Sure you read 'em right, lad?'

'Read 'em yourself, pa,' said Sam mockingly, 'if you don't trust me scholarship.'

'You know I ain't got me spectacles. Just you go on and remember I'm watching.'

So Sam went on and read the names on all the graves—of which there were three and forty—and every man who lay beneath had been taken on that same day of that same year. It was as if the Angel of Death had decided to kill three and forty birds with one stone to save himself the trouble of calling on the village again.

A chill crept over the boy as he stared at the quiet grass and the quiet stones. 'Must have been a storm or something,' he whispered.

'Or something,' repeated his father.

'Plague, maybe?'

'What plague takes only menfolk—and all on the same day?'

'Storm, then, pa.'

'And what storm to reach out and hook 'em all together?'

'Let's find the inn, pa, and ask the landlord.'

His father nodded—then tightened his lips. 'No wild spending, mind.'

'Food and drink, pa. Nothing more.'

'Food I hold with; but not wine.'

'They say Our Lord wasn't against wine, pa—'

'He was the Son of God. You're the son of Job Wilkins. Ale and water for you, lad; and leave the wine be.'

They left the churchyard and walked through the narrow street that twisted among the cottages with many a sharp angle and hiding place for shadows. Sometimes women's faces peered out as they passed; but they looked no more welcoming than had the three fierce children. Being Cornish, they were as sharp and hard as the rocks of their dangerous coast.

At last Job and his son reached the inn, which was the cottage furthest off from the church and had a post outside with a swinging sign of a ship executed as poorly as had been the model in the church. Plainly the villagers had no time for anything but their livelihood from the sea. The father and son pushed open the door and entered directly into the tiny parlour. Ignoring the landlord and his solitary customer, Job made straight for the list of prices that hung in a frame behind the door. 'Read me what it says, lad.'

'We ain't robbers, stranger,' grinned the landlord, not so much to Job as to his scowling customer; 'Parson here'll see you ain't done down.'

The landlord was a short, red-faced man with a remarkably merry expression, like a nutcracker carved out of a very hard wood and coloured and varnished to a high gloss. The parson, on the other hand, was still in a state of nature, so to speak, having a pale, unseasoned complexion with no shine at all save at the tip of his nose which was faintly red as if colouring had been begun and then abandoned as a waste.

'No fish?' said Job, when his son came to the last item on the list which was mutton chops.

'No fish,' confirmed the landlord, nodding his varnished head.

'What becomes of it when it's brought in?'

'Never is, stranger. Never is brought in.'

'Then what do your menfolks do hereabouts?'

'What menfolk, stranger? Have you seen any, maybe?'

'Ain't they out in their boats on this fine day?'

'Yes indeed,' said the parson suddenly coming out of his glass of brandy and setting it down so sharply that the landlord started. 'They're out in their boats all right. Every last one of them. But their boats are long and narrow, each with a lid screwed down tight. And the sea they sail is churchyard earth, with a breaker above of cold grey stone. This is a village of widows, my friends; this is a village that has been damned.'

The parson took up his brandy again, seemed to wash his nose in it, then drank it down. 'They went to hell together, November seven, 1749.'

'Heaven, stranger. Take my word on it,' interposed the cheerful landlord, 'they went in a state of grace; but parson here's fond of his drop of fire and brimstone as he is of his brandy.'

'This is a damned village. Even the sea hates it now,' went on the parson, a holy fire in his faded eyes.

Job shrugged his shoulders and then, in answer to the landlord's inquiry, explained that he and his son were fishermen from the north; but the fish had shifted from their waters so they'd travelled overland in the hopes of finding a better livelihood in the south. The landlord listened with interest and declared that fish had always been plentiful just beyond the bay; and, further, that a widow of his acquaintance owned a capable craft that she'd be willing to rent or sell, if the price proved right.

'Don't listen to him, friends,' warned the parson grimly. 'Better to starve elsewhere than go out from this accursed spot into this accursed sea. At night you can hear it, beating on the shore and cursing it for all eternity.'

'What for?' asked Sam.

'Murder, friend. Foul and hateful murder. When the landlord said fish are plentiful hereabouts, he spoke the truth. No one ever caught them. The sea had a richer harvest. Ships. This was a village of wreckers, my friends.'

There was silence in the little parlour. The landlord had gone to fetch water and ale and the fire danced and spat in the hearth as if in defence of his good name.

'Vessel after vessel they brought onto the rocks with lanterns swung from the headland. And whenever it happened that some poor wretch gained the shore, frantic with relief and thanking God for his escape, they'd murder him as if he'd been no more than a twisting fish. If he wore rings, they'd hack off his fingers before they threw him back into the sea . . .'

The parson stopped as the landlord returned with his unchanging smile. 'Now, now,' he said, setting the jugs of ale and water before Job and his son, 'I don't hold with a churchman speaking against the dead. None of us is perfect and our departed friends may have had their faults. But they went like martyrs and it's certain they went to heaven together. Whatever they might have done in the past, was washed away on that night last year. Judge for yourselves, strangers,' he went on, prodding the fire with his bright boot as if bidding it hold its peace while he talked of the dead. 'Judge for yourselves, and then say honestly whether them three and forty in the graveyard was redeemed or went to roast in hell.

'There was maybe a dozen of us in the parlour that evening. Jacob Tulliver, God rest him, was sitting right where you are, lad.' Hastily, Sam shifted along the bench, and the landlord nodded approvingly, as if he respected Sam's courtesy to a ghost. 'Some of us was playing dice, and there was dominoes on the table in a long, spotted cross. There was no talk of going up on the headland that night, as the weather was calm and fair . . . even as it's been today. So what came to pass was a real act of God, sent to test 'em all. And they came through in glory!'

Here the landlord stared blandly at the parson as if daring him to contradict; but the reverend gentleman contented himself with a holy sneer, so the landlord went on with his calling up of the churchyard sleepers on that fair calm evening of November seven.

Such was his voice and the heated air of the little parlour, together with the weariness of Job and his son, that the dead villagers seemed very real; and as he turned from corner to corner, remembering what they'd said and done, how they'd laughed and bickered and talked over grim old times, Sam could have sworn he felt them jostle him away from the fire . . .

'It had been pretty late; the sun had been down some while and there'd fallen on the parlour one of those queer silences that seem to come at twenty past or twenty to the hour. Some say it's on account of an angel flying overhead. Indeed, Ezra Till made that very observation; so Jacob Tulliver, with a great greasy grin said he'd nip outside and wave to the high flying gentleman. He got up and, being a big man, knocked over a glass on his way.

'He was outside for maybe half a minute,' went on the landlord, staring at the door with a smile that was not so much varnished as frozen, 'when he came back. Burst in with a great commotion. "A ship, a ship!" he shouted. "There's a big ship on the rocks! It's done for, I think!"

'We all rushed out and I remember half the dominoes went flying into the fire. Sure enough, Jacob was right. There was a real monster of a vessel at the end of the bay. She was very high in the poop, like them Spanish or Dutch craft, and she seemed to be hooked for'ard on the rocks; for her stern kept coming round. She was under full sail so it must just have happened . . . though what dozy helmsman could have brought her here out of a calm sea was a mystery.

'Then we heard a shouting far off—a shouting for help; and then the great booming thump as her timbers kept striking on stone. We stood watching for I don't know how long, maybe five minutes, maybe more. The women had come out and the children too, for the night was that clear we could almost make out her name. It was the Santa something . . . but it looked like the sea and the weather had washed out the rest. Then the wind freshened and a parcel of stars was doused. A shadow, like a great hand, fell across the ship and the thumping came quicker and fairly rattled her on the rocks.

‘ “She’s holed!” shouted Ezra, who’d been watching through his glass. “For the love of Jesus! Take a squint, Jacob! I’m going out to her, before all’s lost!”

‘He gave the glass to Tulliver and I can still see the big fellow’s face as the look on it changed as he squinted through it. His greasy grin turned to real passion and pity as if he’d seen dear creatures perishing. “I’m with you, Ezra!” he muttered. “Even if the wind blows straight from hell! Let’s go afore it’s too late!” Then he and Ezra went down for their boat and all the rest followed after.

‘So they went out to that holed ship on the rocks and the wind blew like an iron fist and fair hammered the sea in the bay. But it never stopped them and on they went, hopping over the waves till they was lost from sight in the dark and spray and a ragbag of mist the wind had blown in.’

The landlord paused and shivered as if the sight was still before his eyes. ‘It weren’t till next morning that they came back; and then it was one by one. They came floating, drifting on the tide . . . face down, face up . . . one or two with not much face at all. Pieces of their boats came too—but no more than would have made a rowboat for a child. They’d been smashed on the rocks and drowned—every last one of them. They’d given their lives for that there vessel that cried for help.’

The landlord paused again and stared into the fire that gleamed on his bright cheeks. ‘Judge for yourselves, strangers, whether they wasn’t redeemed by their last acts?’

Before Job and his son could answer, the parson spoke quietly. ‘That was no ordinary ship on the rocks, friends. Neither stitch nor spar of it was ever found; nor did any bodies come ashore save our own three and forty.’

‘It must have got off the rocks and sailed away,’ said the landlord. ‘Tides and currents have done queerer things.’

‘It was holed. It couldn’t have stayed afloat five minutes in the sea,’ said the parson; but the landlord shrugged his stout shoulders and said that whatever became of it was of no consequence. Till and Tulliver had seen something so piteous through the glass that all evil had left them in compassion for it. Thus they perished in a state of grace—

'They went to hell; and it was the devil who fetched them.'

'Then why did they go so eagerly?'

'Who knows what Till and Tulliver saw through their glass?'

'Then give 'em the benefit, parson.'

Thus they argued and pleaded the case for the souls of the three and forty—the parson prosecuting and the landlord defending—as if it rested with the two strangers whether the accused were liberated to heaven or condemned to burn in hell. Little by little the light faded from the sky and still they argued, for none knew what had been seen through the glass that had made three and forty murdering wreckers strike out into the storm and stay in it till the sea cast them back, cold and dead.

'Judge for yourselves, strangers,' repeated the landlord at length, the smile gone from his face and leaving only the shine behind, 'for it's a year ago tonight that they went, and I'm a-thinking they'll be up before the Bench for sentence.' He paused and peered from parson to strangers and then to the fire. A silence fell over the parlour in which the ticking of the mantel clock grew loud. It looked like a small coffin with a white face staring out. The time was twenty after eight. 'An angel's flying overhead,' murmured Sam; when of a sudden, there came another sound . . . a dull booming . . .

All looked to each other in bewilderment; then Job got to his feet and made for the door, upsetting a glass as he did so. A moment later he was back. His heavy face was frowning in alarm. 'A ship,' he muttered. 'There's a ship out in the bay. She's caught on the rocks!'

She was a large vessel, built high in the poop, more Spanish than Dutch, with much gilding that glinted in the starlight. She was under full sail and the huge canvases leaped and cracked at the yards. The dull booming came as her stern kept swinging round and hammering the underwater rocks, for she was caught under her prow . . .

'It's the same ship!' whispered the parson, grey with terror.

'No!' cried the landlord, polishing his forehead with his sleeve as if he felt the varnish cracking. 'It's like, I grant, but it ain't the same vessel. It can't be!'

'Well, whatever it is, we'd best get out to it,' said Job abruptly.

'The same . . . the same . . .' breathed the parson as a dark shadow brushed across the weird ship at the mouth of the bay.

'You said there was a boat,' said Job to the landlord. 'Quick man, let's go before it's too late!'

But there was no crew for the boat save widows, protested the landlord. And the parson supported him, making it as plain as need be that they'd not abandon the inn and the church to go and rescue phantoms from the coming storm.

For the storm was now approaching rapidly. The stars had been put out and the wind had increased so that the distant booming of the ship striking the rock grew more frequent. Faint cries also came in on the wind, and then a sharper, wilder sound.

'She's holed,' muttered Job. 'Did you hear the timbers go, Sammy?'

'You and me, pa,' said Sam with a grin at his father that spoke of a fondness and humour that was fathoms deep. 'We're crew enough!'

The boat was high on the shingle and the widow who owned it came out of her cottage and shook her fist and shrieked into the wind when she saw her property being heaved down to the water by the parson, the landlord and the two bulky strangers. The fierce air tore at her hair and gown till she looked like some thin, wing-stretched bird of ill-omen. Then she caught a glimpse of the huge vessel beating on the rocks. She screamed and covered her face with her hands.

'There's nought of this world about yonder ship, friends!' cried the parson, backing away.

'All the more reason for a parson to come with us!' urged Sam, as the boat began to pull away.

'Save your breath for your oar, Sammy,' grunted Job.

'Right, pa.'

'Keep her steady, Sammy. Go easy.'

'I'm easy, pa. It's you what's puffing.'

'Civil tongue, Sammy, or I'll fetch you one with this oar.'

'No offence, pa.'

'None taken, Sammy; but watch it.'

Thus the father and son, pulling through the dangerous sea, bickered and mocked and provoked each other with a briskness under which lay a deep affection and an unbounded confidence in each other's strength and skill. The little boat rode the great waves with marvellous certainty; and from time to time, Job and Sam, in the midst of some peculiarly sharp exchange, would glance at one another and smile most knowingly . . .

They could only see a short way ahead, for the spray sent up when the bows struck the chests of the waves, hung like grey and silver curtains, screening the recesses of the night. Their chief guide was the dreadful booming of the distressed vessel which now beat in the darkness like the gigantic heart of the sea itself.

'Give a shout, Sammy!'

'Ahoy, there! Stand by for Wilkins and Son!'

'A shout, Sammy, not a squeak. Ain't your voice broke yet?'

'Too much water in me ale, pa. Ahoy, there!'

'There she is, Sammy! What a monster!'

Vague and enormous, the stricken vessel loomed out of the turbulent darkness. Water rushed down the rattling sails in cataracts and poured from the shrouds and yards. She rocked and swung with a mighty uproar like some tremendous carved beast caught in a merciless trap. There was a great hole in her side where a rock had stove her in; but nowhere could Job and Sam see any living souls.

'What's her name, Sammy? Left me spectacles behind.'

The boy lifted his drenched head and peered at the gilded poop.

'Santa—Santa—Can't make out any more . . .'

Then his blood turned chilly as he added, 'It's gone with the weather, pa, like on the signpost.'

'Ahoy there!' shouted Job. 'Come out and be saved! We ain't here for our health!'

'Pa! Pa! Look in the hole! For the love of Jesus, look!'

'Don't blaspheme, Sammy, lad, or—' Then Job saw what Sam had seen, and his jaw fell open, letting in the sea. The hole was amidships and almost on the water line. It yawned like a ragged mouth, and several chests which had slipped their moorings, slid back and forth within it like dim, broken teeth. One

of them had been smashed and out of it there ran a stream of golden coins, that dribbled into the reedy sea.

'Set up for life, pa!' shouted Sam, and pulled on his oar till their boat swung round to approach the leaking gold.

Then, suddenly, there came a faint cry from the darkness to their left. The father and son, poised to go in and collect their fortunes, turned and stared. Briefly they glimpsed a spar, leaping and dipping in the water. A hand was waving.

'Here we go, Sammy.' The boat swung as Wilkins and Son, with one accord, made for the spar. As they did so, the sea drew back from the path they might have taken and revealed a row of rocks with edges like knives. They would have been ripped in two.

They reached the spar. Four men were clinging to it. Their faces were white as bone. 'Care for a trip?' grinned Sam, and reached out to heave them aboard. They were bitterly cold. Their eyes were open but seemed sightless, for an oily film lay across them. Their mouths were gaping, but no words or even breath seemed to issue from them. They were like dead men, and each had his ring finger chopped off below the knuckle. They flopped into the bottom of the boat and lay there while father and son shuddered in bewilderment. But they said nothing to each other of what they thought of their uncanny catch—any more than they'd exchanged words about the danger of the sea. These were private matters and not for the ears of the wind. Instead, they shrugged their shoulders and pulled about and made towards the cargo of gold.

'Quick! Quick! Afore it's all gone!'

'What was that, pa?'

'Never spoke, Sammy. Wash your ears out.'

The boy frowned. The voice he'd heard had been hoarse, urgent and near at hand. 'Pull away, Ezra!' The boy trembled violently, and all but let go of his oar.

'There's ghosts aboard, pa!'

Job looked sideways at his son. 'Then bid 'em lend a hand, Sammy—or fetch 'em one with your oar!'

A second chest aboard the wrecked vessel had cracked open and a river of guineas came dancing out; but again there was heard a faint cry for help from the darkly churning sea.

'Here we go again, Sammy!'

The boy nodded and struggled with his oar. It had become heavier, as if other hands than his were pulling to keep the boat towards the running gold, and away from the cry in the sea. But Sam prevailed and the boat dipped and lifted and swung about till it came alongside a length of planking to which clung three more white-faced men. They also lacked ring fingers and had filmed, sightless eyes. Not knowing to which world they belonged, Job and his son heaved them aboard to join the others who lay, watchful and still at the bottom of the boat.

And again as they'd turned, the sea had drawn back to reveal the murderous rocks that would have sunk them. Then the waves swept high and concealed the danger.

'Third time lucky, pa.'

The gold was pouring out of the queer vessel's side like life's blood. In a few seconds Wilkins and Son could have gathered enough to have been aldermen and respected. As they heaved away, Sam's oar seemed light as a feather—as if other hands than his were helping . . . and the wrecked ship towered in the night.

The wind was lessening, the sea lost its sharp edges and rolled in thick, smooth folds. A mist was coming in, dense and grey. Already the masts and sails were eaten up in the vapours and the high gilding of the poop was partly nibbled away.

'Make haste, Sammy—'

But Job's words were interrupted by a weird chorus of cries—like an anthem of despair.

'Yonder, Sammy; yonder!'

The boy stared hard to where his father pointed . . . and shuddered to the depths of his soul. As the sea rolled dark and oily under the heavy folds of mist, he saw what seemed to be a vast coverlet of men, women and children rising and falling in a weird, slow dance. Hundreds and hundreds of them, with bone-white faces gleaming like bubbles on the wave.

'God in heaven, pa!'

'That's as maybe, Sammy; but we're down below. Let's do what we can, boy!'

So once again they turned from fortune, and once again Sam shut his ears to the hoarse voices that pleaded, 'The gold! The gold!'

'Women and children, Sammy!' panted Job as they nosed among the floating crowd. Then Wilkins and Son began to fill the little boat till it seemed that they must all sink under the weight. They dragged and heaved and piled them in—and Sam saw, with nightmarish terror, that there was not a whole hand anywhere among them. Fingers were gone, even from children.

At last they were stacked so thick and high that there was scarce room to row, when Sam heard a soft scream almost in his ear. 'Jacob Tulliver! They've come for us! There's the child I killed last week! And there's the mother that cried so afore you knocked her on the head! Look—look! All of them!'

'Pa!' howled Sam, feeling the unnatural chill of their cargo pressing against his legs, his back and his neck. 'They're all ghosts! They're the ghosts of them the wreckers murdered!'

'That's as maybe, Sammy,' answered Job, pale of face and stern of eye. 'But ghosts or otherwise, we ain't got room for any gold now. It's back to the shore, lad!'

They turned and began to row through the all engulfing mists towards where Job's unfailing instinct told him the shore lay. As they moved blindly across the foggy sea, Sam heard distinct shrieks and howls and the splitting of timber on rock as the phantoms of the three and forty wreckers foundered again, even as they'd foundered a year ago that night, under the tempting stream of gold.

'Looks like the parson was right, pa!' panted Sam. 'Looks like they went to hell like he said!'

'Like as you said before, Sammy,' grunted Job, 'God's in His heaven; and like I said, we're down below. Where that three and forty went is none of your business or mine. Don't go poking your nose in, boy; just keep rowing.'

The fog was now so dense that Job and Sam were almost hidden from each other, and their uncanny cargo, stirring, sighing and muttering, was no longer seen. Presently the motion of the boat was arrested and the keel whispered on sand. They had reached the shore.

'Ahoy, there!' shouted Job, for the air was thick as wool. There came an answering shout and at length the landlord, the parson and the bony widow came stumbling out of the nothingness to stare incredulously at the returned strangers.

'Never thought to see you back!' was the landlord's greeting, as he heaved to bring the boat clear of the sea.

'What was it, friends? What was that terrible ship, and what was it those damned souls saw that drew them out to destruction? For they were damned, weren't they?'

'Can't say, parson,' answered Job, shaking the sea off his arms and out of his thick grey hair. 'Left me spectacles behind.' He stared severely at Sam whose mouth had opened as if to confirm the parson's words.

'The mist's lifting,' said the landlord turning his gleaming face out to sea. 'Comes and goes in these parts with marvellous speed.'

The little group on the shore stared as the air grew thin and clean again. The great ship had vanished; neither spar nor stitch of canvas remained to be seen. Uneasily Sam looked into their boat. He sighed. The fearful catch for which they'd turned from fortune and risked their lives had shrunk. In place of the ghostly murdered dead lay a heap of faintly shining mackerel whose filmy eyes stared back at him.

'It was a phantom ship!' ranted the parson, his eyes burning with brandy and holy fire. 'And they all went to hell with it! This place is accursed.'

'There was souls in the sea,' murmured Job softly, 'and maybe they was phantoms too. And maybe your three and forty went out to fetch 'em in. Ain't it possible?'

'Pa!' cried Sam, who'd good cause to know otherwise. 'They—' He got no further, for Job Wilkins clipped him smartly round the ear.

'Speak when you're spoke with, Sammy boy!'

'So—so they might have been redeemed?' whispered the landlord, polishing his forehead as if he meant to exhibit it.

'As like as maybe,' nodded Job, eyeing the heap of mackerel. 'At all events, the sea hereabouts is mighty rich, I'd say; and with your permission, ma'am' (to the widow), 'Sam and me'll come back with Mrs. Wilkins and be happy to take a lease on your vessel—if the price is right.'

'You're lying my friends,' said the parson when they were back in the inn and drying off before the fire. 'I know you saw what really happened that night a year ago. Come, admit it. Say they were damned and this placed is accursed.'

But Job did not seem to hear him. He'd gone to the little window and gazed out towards the church. There was a splinter of moon and under it the village slept in silver dreams; while the three and forty graves in the churchyard seemed to have broken ranks . . . as if their long parade had finished and they might lie easy.

'This here's a pretty village,' murmured Job to Sam. 'What call have the dead to curse it, so long as we don't curse them? Rest easy, gents. If you wasn't redeemed last year, it's as like as maybe you are now. Eh. Sammy?'

'Right, pa.'